PRASE .... ARLND

"Vivian Arend does a wonderful job of building the atmosphere and the other characters in this story so that readers will be sucked into the world and looking forward to the rest of the books in the series."
~ *Library Journal*

"Steamy and sweet complete with a whole host of colourful side characters and enough sub-plots to get your teeth into. A fab read!"
~ *Scorching Book Reviews*

"There's a real chemistry between the characters, laced with humor and snappy dialogue and no shortage of steamy sex scenes to keep things lively. The result is an entertaining, spicy romance."
~ *Publishers Weekly*

I have honestly waited AGES for Vivian to return to her world of shifters and this new trilogy is just what the Romance Witch doctor ordered! The setting is beautiful, the characters are hilarious, and the best friends-to-lovers story never gets old...
~ *Romance Witch Reviews*

Arend offers constant action and thrills, and her characters are so captivating and nuanced that readers will have a hard time guessing who the villains really are.
~ *RT Book Reviews*

THE BEAR'S FOREVER MATE

BOREALIS BEARS: BOOK 3

VIVIAN AREND

The Bear's Forever Mate
Copyright © 2020 by Arend Publishing Inc.
ISBN: 9781999495794
Edited by Anne Scott
Cover Design © Damonza
Proofed by Angie Ramey, Linda Levy, & Manuela Velasco

Personal Journal, Giles Borealis, Sr.

And so one remains.

Of course, it makes sense that he'd be the final one to follow my instructions and find himself a mate. Stubborn as the day is long, just like his father.

Like every male member of this family, if we're being honest.

Cooper's probably the most like me when it comes down to it. Protective, caring—he's a solid rock for the rest of the family. The lad's always got one of his brothers coming to him for advice, and in any group, everyone seems to gravitate in his direction.

He strives to do the right thing for everyone else. Damn well time he did the right thing for himself for a change.

Stubborn boy would argue about that, I'm sure. Legal training never goes amiss except when the young varmints try to use it to wiggle their way out of losing a discussion with me.

Don't know why he thinks he can continue to get away with being so perverse. He got that character trait from some other side of the family. Possibly from my beloved mate, although I'd never tell Laureen my suspicions.

Anyway, I know the type of woman Cooper needs. She's got to have a soft touch to slip in under that protective instinct of his, but a spine of steel to force his hand when he gets all unreasonable. Amber is definitely the one for him, and between her and the mating fever, there's no way Cooper will get away.

So, yes, my oldest grandson will fall as well, no matter how firmly he believes the contrary. I set the wheels in motion for this match so long ago, he'll never see it coming. Won't know that I was involved at all.

Which is right, I suppose. I don't have to get the credit for making fine matches for my grandsons. I just want the grandbabies for me and Laureen to cuddle, and if I read the signs right, this last match might end up being the perfect beginning to the next generation.

Getting older means I have the time to watch their stories unfold. I can hardly wait to see what Christmas brings to the Borealis family, and most especially to Cooper and Amber.

I won't gloat until everything is completed, but it's coming—

I can tell!

INTERLUDE

December. A remote cabin, somewhere in the wilds of the Canadian Northwest Territories.

*C*ooper Borealis tightened his grip on the window frame and fought for control.

I don't know why you need to complicate everything, his inner bear complained. *It's the mating fever, not the guillotine.*

There are reasons. I've explained this before. You're not human, so you don't get it, but this is important. Remember your promise.

Talking with the shifter side of himself was as natural as breathing, but right here? Right now? Cooper was borderline tipping into the disaster zone, and explanations needed to remain short and sweet.

Another wave of sexual need rolled through his system, and he shuddered as he turned away from the winter scene. Early that morning he'd retreated to this small cabin, and it was now time to lock up so that he didn't do something unwise like leave and track down the woman he wanted.

The woman he intended to be with When The Time Was Right. Which was about five years from now. Maybe a little sooner if he and Amber Myawayan could deal with all the issues standing in their way before then.

A low growl rumbled inside, and Cooper sensed he was reaching the end of his leash. No problem...

Well, lots of potential problems, but fewer if his polar bear half behaved.

You remember your promise? Cooper asked yet again.

That is amazingly annoying, the beast snapped. *Why do you think I have the attention span of a gnat when I'm part of you and I assume you don't think* you're *incompetent?*

Just need you to understand this is serious, Cooper repeated.

He sat on the bed and double-checked that everything he needed was within reach. A cooler of food, plenty of water. He tugged the length of chain that lay across the floor, the shiny links reaching toward the bathroom then looping back to the bed. The heavy-metal restraining system was long enough so he could deal with being trapped for the duration of the fever without hurting himself.

Yet the chain was short enough he couldn't reach the door or leave. It was as perfect as this wild situation could be.

As long as his bear didn't use his strength to break free.

Cooper linked the handcuff around his left wrist. *You promised to stay out of the picture while the mating fever runs its course. You will not take control of the shift and break the cuff. You will not—*

I will kick your ass if you continue to lecture me like I'm a five-year-old cub. I heard your explanation of why you don't want to enjoy the fever, yet again, and while I think you're a few fish short of a barrel, I promised. Now Shut. Up. You're pissing me off.

Communications with his shifter side choked to a halt like a tap had been closed.

It appeared the damn beast was pouting.

Cooper shrugged then tightened the cuff, tugging slightly to make sure his human strength wasn't enough to break the chain free from its anchor on the bed frame. He was a big man, and it wasn't impossible that he'd be able to wrench himself free from a normal bed and cuff.

Which was why he'd made sure to have the Necessary Upgrades To The Safe House installed when he'd booked the cabin.

When even a sharp tug held against the metal reinforcements, Cooper lay on the mattress and closed his eyes.

Mating fever had arrived.

His thoughts tangled as sexual need and the urge to track down the object of his desire flared again. This time Cooper didn't fight the images flashing to his brain.

Amber, her dark hair falling over one shoulder as she looked up at him from lowered lashes.

The only woman he wanted, her sweater falling open to reveal naked skin at her shoulder and the upper curve of her breast.

The beautiful Japanese-Canadian woman staring at him, her eyes dark and full of concern as she leaned in close. Her knees rested on the bed beside him, far enough away she had pressed a hand to his naked chest to balance.

An odd sensation soaked through his feverish thoughts. The pressure on his chest was real.

Oh my God, he was having a heart attack. This denying the fever was going to be the literal death of him.

Cooper snapped his eyes open to discover the dark eyes, the knees on the mattress, and the sexy woman perched over him were not products of his fevered imagination.

Amber was really there.

Oh, damn...

1

Two weeks earlier, Yellowknife, Northwest Territories

The lights in the room over the Diamond Tavern were all on, the rich yellow and gold fighting off the winter darkness.

Cooper finished his first glass of whiskey then refilled his drink before leaning back in his chair. He ignored the antique clock on the wall that was about to sound the top of the hour.

His brothers were late for their weekly meeting. Again.

Although he supposed he couldn't blame them. Both his younger siblings had ladies at home now who were keeping them on their toes—

Laughter rang from somewhere downstairs. A hearty sound from Alex that was echoed by James. Satisfaction and happiness that screamed they'd not only found companionship but sexual contentment with their mates.

The image of deep brown eyes and the softest fall of long dark hair shot through Cooper's brain along with the scent of *her*. His body reacted instantly, and he stretched

7

out his legs to create more room. He couldn't even blame animal instincts—this was all human reaction to one huge temptation.

A moment later the door to his right swung open and Amber Myawayan poked her head out. "I finished the final tasks you wanted sorted. Need anything else before I head home?"

What did he need? To pick her up and lick the pulse at the base of her neck would be a good starting point. Or maybe to wrap his hands around her waist and place her on top of his desk, after he'd stripped every inch of clothing from her body, then lay her out to feast on the sweetness betwee—

Cooper shook his head firmly as his brothers stepped into the room. "Nothing, thanks."

"Then I'll see you tomorrow." She smiled at Alex and James as she weaved past them, walking out the door and taking Cooper's heart with her.

His bear lunged.

Cooper hauled the beast back under control. *Not yet.*

But you want her, his bear grumbled.

Patience, Cooper scolded.

You know we hate being patient, his bear stated plainly. *Patience sucks.*

Indeed, it did.

"Hey, Amber. I almost forgot. Send Kaylee a text," James called after her as he settled in his chair kitty-corner to Cooper's. "She wants to coordinate something with you."

"Will do." Her answer drifted up the stairs, her voice growing fainter.

"I hope there's more of that left," Alex said with a gesture toward Cooper's drink. He grinned as he spotted the whiskey bottle and headed over to pour servings for

8

himself and James. "That's something I like about you, Coop. Always prepared, especially in the important things."

Cooper smiled in acknowledgement of the compliment. "It's one of my many talents."

His younger brothers lifted their glasses in a toast before they all took a slow sip. Appreciative noises sounded from Alex and James immediately, which Cooper admitted was deeply satisfying.

He liked being good at what he did, whether it was running the family gem company or choosing fine liquors. No use doing a job if you were going to only do it half-assed.

Cooper Borealis was not the type to half-ass anything.

"Either of you heard from Mom and Dad lately?" James put forward the question, his eyes bright with contentment as he propped up his feet and relaxed.

Alex shook his head. "The last update said they plan to Skype with us sometime before the end of the year, but they were headed into an area with no internet service. I don't expect more news until just before New Year's. They would never miss Gramps's birthday celebration, even if it's just a virtual visit."

"Kaylee's parents will still be MIA during the holidays. Which isn't all bad." James made a face as he whirled his whiskey thoughtfully. "I guess that means Christmas dinner will be the five of us, plus Grandpa and Grandma."

Amber should come too, his bear suggested.

His inner beast had opinions. Cooper constantly had to explain to his other half how the real world worked, because the bear side of him didn't seem to understand logic and reasoning, at least not beyond a certain point. It wasn't that he was childish—his animal side was wicked smart—but... innocent perhaps. His suggestions were not always human appropriate.

She's not family, Cooper said smoothly. *Holiday gatherings are for family.*

She's almost family, the beast returned. *She knows everyone, knows everything, and she's around all the time.*

Trust me, this is a human thing. I know she's around a lot, but that doesn't make her family. Holidays are for immediate family only, unless we all decide otherwise. No matter that someday Cooper fully intended for Amber to be included in the family, the time had not yet arrived.

Human rules make no sense, his bear commented dryly. *You don't understand logic.*

Logic makes no sense if it means no Amber.

Okay, Cooper couldn't argue with that.

While he'd been chatting with his inner bear, Alex and James had continued to discuss holiday plans. James nodded then filled Cooper in. "If Grandma and Grandpa agree, we'll all head over to their place for Christmas day. It's not as if we don't get together on a regular basis for meals, but since this is a bigger deal, Alex is in charge of the gift exchange, and Kaylee said she'd coordinate the food. We'll all chip in so Grandma isn't stuck with all the work."

"Time's running short on another matter." Alex was the one who said it, but both his brothers wore serious expressions as they turned to examine Cooper.

"Grandpa's letter said we had to have things settled before the end of the year. The mating fever and all." James considered then his face brightened. "Hey, I just thought of something. Didn't the fever last hit you in early January? Maybe you won't get it until then, which means Grandpa won't be able to hold you to your promise since he didn't issue the challenge until March. He's supposed to finalize the ownership papers by the end of *this* year, yes?"

Cooper had already considered that. "It might be a

valid escape clause, but I'll be ready, no matter what. Don't worry, I won't do anything to jeopardize what you've both accomplished."

Although he had plenty of his own plans and hopes, their grandfather's demand the three of them give in to the mating fever this year or lose control of the family business had forced Cooper's hand. His list of How To Settle Down In The Most Advantageous And Pleasurable Manner had been kicked into overdrive before he wanted.

Alex had attempted to control fate by picking the worst possible match when the fever hit him. James had picked the best—his best friend. Cooper was more like his youngest brother, and also had someone in mind. She would be perfect...

...in about five years. They had way too much to work through before Cooper could slide into action mode and sweep Amber off her feet.

Want her? Definitely, but the fact he was her boss was the simplest of their complications.

He had *all* the obstacles cataloged, of course. Defined and delineated in the Barriers To Potential Mating Bliss list.

Fortunately, having dealt with the mating fever on a regular basis over the past ten years, Cooper had a little more ammunition when it came to facing the fever *and* keeping his promise to his brothers regarding the ultimatum Grandfather had issued.

The page in his notebook dedicated to that topic was titled "Surviving The Fever Without Fucking Up."

Titling his lists wasn't always easy, and the simple truth usually worked best.

No, as much as he enjoyed the time with his siblings, Cooper knew there were a million ways this could go wrong, but if he was very, very careful, and very determined, he'd be able to get himself and Amber through the next month or so without the world imploding.

Once ownership of Borealis Gems was safely settled, and once he'd kept his word to his brothers... Once the fever was done and gone, and the *other* barriers between him and Amber were taken care of...

Then he would go after her with a dogged determination. A *polar bear*-ed determination.

Something poked him in the hand. He blinked to attention to discover Alex standing over him, smacking a sheaf of papers against his palm.

Cooper opened it to find a list of security protocols Alex had organized for upcoming holiday events. An identical list already sat on his main office desk where the very efficient Amber had placed it earlier that afternoon. "What's this?"

"You called and asked for an update." Alex frowned as he sat back down. "You headed into hibernation mode, bro? You're not the brightest bulb right now."

James's eyes opened wide, and he leaned in, a thrill in his tone. "Is it the fever?"

"No, it's not the damn fever, and we don't hibernate. Jerks." Cooper wadded the papers into a ball and tossed it at the garbage, shaking his head when the paper ricocheted off the rim to land in a crumpled heap on the floor.

"You need to work on your game, Coop," James teased.

"My game is just fine." Or it would be. Cooper would be sure of that. In all its variations.

Now was the time for patience and logic and, above all else, to avoid being caught alone with the delectable Amber Myawayan.

Games? You want to play games? his inner bear drawled.

Don't get involved, Cooper warned. *This is human stuff.*

I wouldn't dream of interfering. Human games are for humans. I'll stick to what bears do best.

No way was he touching that one, because frankly? He didn't want to know what mischief his beast planned to cause. There was only one response for here and now.

Cooper tipped back his full glass of whiskey and drained it in one go.

2

*D*arkness lay over the land, tucked into the valleys and trees like a warm blanket. The winter night air was crisp and clear, and snow covered the ground in thick layers. Overhead, the brilliant northern lights danced, and their shining brightness offered a softness and a sort of magic to the evening.

Amber would accept all the magic she could get if it helped her reach her dreams.

"Sorry I was late." The woman at her side, Kim, apologized for the umpteenth time.

Amber waved the comment off yet again, allowing her amusement to come through clearly in her tone as she steered the company's massive four-wheel drive toward their destination. "It's no trouble," she insisted. "I love watching the aurora borealis, and giving you a ride makes it easier for me to justify being out of the office tomorrow morning since I worked late tonight."

Kim laughed softly. "I'm just glad not to miss..."

Ahead of them, the entire night sky lit up.

The woman's words faded into a soft sigh of wonder,

palms braced on her knees as she leaned forward. Her gaze was fixed on the ever-changing rolling lights, and her jaw hung open in amazement.

Amber knew the sensation well. It took discipline to keep her gaze on the road, because the northern lights were one of the biggest miracles she'd ever witnessed.

She pulled into the parking lot and the space reserved for Borealis Gems owners and staff. "Let's get you reunited with your husband. He's going to be happy you made it after all."

Winter chill surrounded them on the short walk to the cozy warming hut. Small lights set at ground level lit the snow without making the darkness overly bright. The back door to the beautiful building was welcoming, lit by two softly glowing lamps, but the specialized construction kept the inside of the building dark from floor to ceiling. The blackness created a wonderful viewing gallery for those who found being out in the elements too much.

"We go this way," Amber instructed, because while the hut was an option, that wasn't where the real tour began, and she didn't expect Kim's husband to be waiting under the roof for her.

A group of shifters who had come to view the northern lights? Outside all the way.

Amber turned the corner and spotted *him*. Cooper, the source of so many fantasies and longings. Tall and solid with killer arms that had inspired her to reposition her desk to gain a better line of site. Now she spent her days covertly watching for the moment he'd get lost in his task and unthinkingly roll up his sleeves, baring said killer forearms.

A sigh escaped before she could stop it.

The entire man was amazing—from his silver-tipped black hair down to the muscular legs not at all hidden in his business suit. His expensive clothes were tailored to fit his long body, and he *was* a beautiful man.

But those *arms*—the oh-so-sexy forearms with a dusting of hair that reflected silver in the light. A trick of nature sneaking in from his animal side? Amber wasn't certain.

She hadn't had a lot of chances to spend one-on-one time with the wild side of many shifters, although she was good friends with Kaylee, who was a bobcat shifter.

She *wanted* time to get to know Cooper better. Both halves, man and bear.

If she could only get him to acknowledge her before she was forced to jot down *All Amber's Positive Qualities* in one of his damn notebooks herself.

Not that she'd ever peeked in his private journals. She'd been tempted, hugely, but some things were off-limits. Maybe once they'd been together for a few years, or years and years, and after he'd given her carte blanche, then she'd be willing to delve into his private thoughts.

Because, yes, she intended to reach that point. The only reason she knew about his "Important Thoughts Deserve Capitals" habit was because he did it all the time for work. He was not the type to change methods in midstream, especially not when they were successful.

She deliberately gathered her courage and stepped forward, Kim pacing at her side. The other woman was still mesmerized by the natural light show overhead, but her gaze flickered from the sky to the area in front of them.

"Mrs. Wayne. So glad you could make it." Cooper spoke politely with that dash of intensity that made the recipient feel as if they were the only person on the face of the earth.

Or, Amber thought, maybe that was her damn obsession with the man shining through.

"Amber was kind enough to pick me up after I missed the first van." Kim tilted her head toward Amber and offered a grateful smile. Then she turned back to Cooper. "Would you know where Bruce is? I have a surprise for him."

"He and the rest of the company just stepped around the corner to get more comfortable."

Kim fluttered her fingers at Amber then took off eagerly to rejoin her group.

And then it was the two of them. Amber and Cooper, standing beside the warming hut with a stunning display of nature shimmering overhead and their own private viewing station.

She twisted until she could stare into his face and offer her best smile. "Looks like a spectacular night."

Cooper clasped his hands behind his back, gaze tilted upward. The dancing lights reflected in his eyes, turning them into living kaleidoscopes. "There's never a bad evening while watching the northern lights."

"True." She stepped a little nearer, tucking her coat around herself more firmly, as if blaming the move toward him on the icy November wind curling around them. "Everything's better with the right people, though."

For a second she thought this was it. The moment she'd been longing for. His breathing quickened, and he leaned closer—maybe because he was going to admit that he and she, together, were *right people*?

Because she could've sworn that over the past two years she wasn't the only one who had become interested in exploring a deeper relationship. Yes, she'd worked for him, laughing at his droll humour and admiring his work ethic. But it was the way he cared for his family with stubborn good intentions that had been the kicker. Two years meant she'd learned enough about the man that she admired him through and through. He was someone she could grow to feel very affectionate toward...

Screw being diplomatic. Cooper was *exactly* the kind of man she wanted to fall in love with. Even blunter—she was halfway there, or more, already.

She was certain he'd grown equally interested in her, but getting the big growly bear to admit anything was like teaching someone how to fasten snowshoes in the dark.

Beyond awkward and not very successful.

"The right people? Definitely." He lifted his arm and examined his watch for a moment before tapping a short message then resuming his statue-like position. "We have good friends and good family here in the north. And I know our guests certainly enjoy getting to share the experience with each other."

She was tempted to growl at him. That wasn't what she meant at all.

A spectacular roll of light went off overhead, and they both grew silent. No matter how important her agenda, there were some moments no one should interrupt.

Five minutes passed as they stood in comfortable silence. Amber had just decided it was time to try a different tack, when around the side of the building came the strangest apparition. It took a second to figure out what, or more specifically *who*, was there. It was Kim. The long-legged blonde dashed across the snowy expanse in her bare feet, her long hair trailing her like a banner.

She wasn't naked—that would've been less startling. Instead, the woman wore a bikini that somehow reflected the lights as they appeared overhead in the northern sky. Blues and greens floated across her boobs, and a flash of neon purple slid across her hip and between her legs, as if the aurora borealis overhead had wrapped itself around Kim's torso in an embrace.

"What on earth...?" Cooper began, before his words faded into nothing.

The woman ran, laughter lilting in the air even as she glanced over her shoulder. A large bear was hot on her heels. Not as if it were intent on fighting for territory. No, this was most definitely a shifter thing. The big bear's gait was more prance-y than menacing, and he bounced a few times like a kangaroo before changing direction and herding Kim toward the trees.

Amber shivered. Not reacting was impossible. She knew very well what was going to happen when Bruce caught her. Shifters were lusty creatures, and between mates there was no need for holding back.

Not to mention that *humans* often took off to semiprivate places to enjoy sex under the shimmering aurora borealis—rumours of the magic offered by the lights were a part of many northern cultures. The stories had been shared around the world until they were somewhere between legend and truth, and impossible to ignore.

The magical good fortune supposedly waiting for couples who partook in *intimate* activities was enough to make even the most reserved consider a little outdoor entertainment.

Amber's heart rate jumped a notch. Sex. Outdoors. With Cooper.

Yes. Yes, *yes.*

Her pulse kicked up even faster when Cooper's hand landed on her shoulder, and he pulled her against his side. Oh my goodness, was he finally going to—

He patted her gently as if soothing a frightened child.

"It's okay," he assured her. "They're shifters. She's not cold. And Bruce isn't going to hurt her."

"I know that." She leaned against his side and looked up. Please, let him read in her expression what she found so difficult to put into words. *I would very much like to be rolling around under the northern lights with you.*

He examined her face, his gaze pausing for a second on her mouth, and in that instant, her dreams trembled on the verge of coming true...

He tapped her on the nose as if she were a puppy then glanced over her shoulder. "Hey, look who's here."

She blinked at the abrupt change. Mind still clouded with desire and mightily confused, she followed his lead and twisted to discover familiar company marching across the snow toward them. Her best friend Kaylee and her mate, James. And Cooper's other brother, Alex, with his wolf partner, Lara.

Kaylee stared upward in amazement as James guided her forward. "Wow, Cooper, you were right. It is a spectacular evening. Thanks for messaging us to let us know."

So that was what he'd been tapping on his watch for. Calling in his family. It was something she loved about him —how clearly important his family was to him.

Frustrating when they blocked her plans, though.

"Hey, guys." Amber put as much enthusiasm into the words as she could fake. Another opportunity lost.

Kaylee wrapped an arm around Amber and cuddled her tight before slipping aside to plant a kiss on James that sent up howling from the rest of their group.

Amber's friend smiled sweetly. "Sorry for the PDA, but there's something about spectacular nights like this that makes me feel all tingly and alive."

A snort of amusement escaped Alex. He and Lara had just finished a brief whispered conversation. They exchanged a grin before deliberately turning their backs toward the open field. With her hyper-sensitive wolf hearing, Lara probably knew exactly what was happening in the trees right now.

"Feeling *tingly* seems to be a common theme amongst the visitors tonight. What's going on, bro?" Alex asked Cooper. "Did you bring in a group of naturalists?"

Amber peeked toward the field, but Cooper stepped in her way, blocking whatever cavorting might be visible. "Just some high spirits. Come on, guys. It's too cold out here for Amber. I've got a bottle of the good stuff waiting for us inside the hut."

The cheers that prompted meant there was no use in Amber explaining she wasn't really cold. Just like there was no use in explaining that if she were, the way she wanted to be warmed up was in the big bear's arms.

But she smiled and followed along, joining her friends to enjoy the show even as she plotted her new plan of attack.

Before this year was out, she and Cooper were going to have A Very Important And Blunt Discussion. Maybe it was time to call in the reinforcements she'd been promised to make that happen.

One way or another, she needed to gather her courage and pin down her bear. She didn't want to waste another moment.

3

---

*Items To Be Accomplished Prior To Succumbing To The
Mating Fever*
•review next year's second quarter projections
•purchase chain and appropriate Alex's handcuffs
•year-end message for shareholders
•meet with R&D
•avoid being alone with Amber at all costs

"*We*'re going to find it really hard to win this thing if you've got your nose stuck in that notebook," James grumbled.

"You're going to find it hard to win since you're competing against the best of the best," came Alex's instant response from a few feet away.

A chorus of cheers and jeers rose from the crowd behind him—a motley crew of wolves from the Orion pack house.

Lara rolled her eyes then tossed a glare over her shoulder. "Children, behave."

"But we *are* going to win," one of them quipped. The

lanky young man, Dixon, adjusted his red and white *Where's Waldo?* toque so the red ball of fluff on the tip stuck up jauntily, his white teeth flashing against tan skin.

"Of course we are, Dix," Lara agreed. "But you don't have to gloat about it."

"Yet." Alex ducked the snowball James tossed at him, only to step directly into the path of Kaylee's missile. His expression of dismay vanished behind a smear of white. When he reopened his eyes, it was to grin evilly at his sister-in-law. "Game on, lady."

Chaos. Absolute and completely wonderful family-flavoured chaos swirled around Cooper. He tucked his notebook inside his coat pocket and zipped it closed so he could give his full attention to the afternoon's festivities.

At noon, the sun was up and as high as it was going to get on this early December day, which meant not very. It offered a cold light that shone on the playground of the local high school where they'd gathered for today's special event.

Every year, a highly competitive ice sculpture contest was held in Yellowknife. Contestants from around the world entered, and the sculptures were miracles of ice and snow.

A couple years earlier a special community-based version had been started specifically for the high school students. Run a few months before the official event, it was a combination of a pre-holiday adrenaline burner for the youth and a plain good time.

It had been Amber's idea—because of course it had.

The sponsoring teams for the event were Borealis Gems and Midnight Inc., with a collection of representatives from each company joining the students to help create works of art out of glistening ice. It was all in fun. The prizes were mostly funding given to the various sports and arts groups in the school that needed an infusion of money.

Everyone joined in, learned new skills, and when the sun went down and the contest was over, they ate pizza. Lots and lots of pizza and chips and other junk food, because that was just the kind of party it was.

Grandfather Giles clapped his hands as he stepped forward, motioning in the stragglers from the far corners of the field.

He glanced around at the eager faces. After dodging a snowball, then offering Alex a warning glare, he raised his voice far above what the average eighty-four-year-old should be able to achieve. There was nothing frail about the man, his back unbowed and eyes bright. Only the silvery white in his hair and beard hinted at his age.

"We're glad you're all here today. I'm not going to waste a lot of time blabbing at you. The rules are simple—you've all been assigned a block of ice and teams of two or more. Everyone needs to participate as you produce your creative masterpiece. Anyone who needs help or wants a power tool assist, give a shout, and one of the sponsors for your team will come by to see what they can do." He offered Grandmother Laureen a grin paired with a mischievous wink. "My lovely wife and I will be the final judges. You've got three hours. Have fun."

A burst of energy lit up the snow-packed field as teenagers exploded outward in a rush. Groups of two and three scattered across the field to gather around the massive ice blocks that had been set up. Some on tables, some free-standing that were as tall as Cooper.

"You'd better go get started," Alex taunted. "The sooner you begin, the sooner I can beat you."

"He's awfully cocky," James noted, arms wrapped

around his mate as she pulled on a thick pair of fuzzy mittens.

"I've noticed that about your brother," Kaylee offered dryly. "One danger of living in the pack house. He's getting more wolflike by the minute."

Cooper pointed them toward a group of three teenagers who were already waving their hands. Alex and Lara had headed in the opposite direction, hand in hand as they rejoined the wolves who were working with their assigned teams.

"Time you got to work as well," Grandfather Giles said as he settled Grandmother on one of the two chairs set up like a royal dais, then took the other throne. "Much as I hate to admit it, that Midnight Inc. crew has some talented artists. Borealis Gems needs to put in a good show, or your grandmother and I will have no choice but to award all the prizes to our rivals."

Cooper ignored the older man for a moment, instead turning to look questioningly at Grandmother Laureen. "I thought you were going to be my partner."

She sighed heavily. "My arthritis is acting up, so I agreed to judge instead. Don't worry. I found a replacement. She'll be here soon."

An uneasy feeling welled in Cooper's stomach. "She?"

The answer arrived at that moment. Amber popped out from behind the fence and headed straight for them.

This was not good for so many reasons.

"Grandmother," Cooper scolded mildly. "Carving tools are dangerous if you don't know what you're doing."

One perfect brow arched upward as his grandmother stared him down. Usually it was his grandfather who made Cooper mind his p's and q's, but right now it was clear Grandmother Laureen was having none of his nonsense.

She sniffed. "I don't think you have anything to worry about."

"It's just that—"

Disapproval scalded him. "Trust me, Cooper," his grandmother said mildly. "And be polite. She gave up her day off to replace me."

Amber waved hello, the other hand occupied with a boxlike carrying case. "Hello. I got here as quick as I could."

"They've just begun," Grandfather Giles assured her then turned to his wife and spoke quietly, his gaze intent as if they were talking about a thing of vital importance and not to be interrupted.

Cooper glanced at Amber's bright face. The notebook in his pocket pulsed a warning signal. The list he'd just gone over that said that being alone with her in any capacity was a dangerous thing.

The one that reminded him that the last time they'd been partly alone she'd shivered with fear at a modest display of sexual playfulness between shifters. What was going to happen when he finally did make a move? Would she run from him, and not in a good way?

Her smile faded, and he realized he'd been staring without moving as his brain worked overtime.

"Something wrong?" she asked quietly.

There was no way to deal with this other than bluffing his way through. They were in a public place, wearing five layers of clothing—she was, at least. Of course they could spend time together without him giving in to the animal urges that continued to grow inside.

Heh. Animal inside. Don't you think that's a little clichéd?

Cooper wanted to bang his head against the nearest

wall, but there wasn't one readily available. *Please don't start on me today.*

You need to learn to relax, his bear taunted. *Animals are good at relaxing. Maybe if you curled up with a sweet little thing who smells like heaven—*

It wasn't easy to put a chokehold on his bear *and* force a smile, but he did it so he could answer Amber without growling. Or jumping her. Jumping would be really bad.

Difference of opinion on that one, his inner beast grumbled a half second before vanishing in a huff.

Smile. Focus on the smile. "The change of plans threw me for a moment, but I've got it now."

She was still examining him with unease, so he focused on all the things she did that made his life easier, instead of how much he was looking forward to being able to share his other feelings with her somewhere down the road. Real warmth had to have reached his expression because the concern on her face faded.

Amber nodded decisively. "Come on, let's go see who needs help."

Around them, students donned safety gear then dove into their projects. New shapes appeared as the edges of the blocks were cut off, slivers of ice raining down in miniature snowstorms. With only three hours to work, no one was going to be able to finish anything hugely detailed, and they all knew that.

Creativity and boldness would be rewarded.

Cooper paused beside a table where three girls had turned their block into a triangle-shaped object with a large bulge on one side. Two of the girls were making faces while the third spoke rapidly, her hands moving in an attempt to describe what she thought needed to happen next.

One of the girls shook her head, turning to Cooper and

Amber. "It sort of makes sense, but I don't see how we can do it without ruining the entire piece of ice."

Cooper hesitated. He wasn't sure how to help with their idea, either.

Amber placed the box she'd been carrying on the table beside them, listening carefully as the third girl tried again to explain. "I see your problem."

She flipped open the case and pulled out what looked a lot like an electric knife. It was—and a noticeably powerful one. She hit the *on* button and quickly moved to the front of the triangle.

A couple cuts later the girls were nodding excitedly, their voices rising with eager suggestions.

But Amber turned off the tool and pointed to what they had to work with. "Now that I've got you started, carry on."

Instead of a vague triangle with a lumpy bump, the clear outline of a necklace lay against a display shelf. A very suitable project for a contest sponsored by two diamond companies.

The girls went to work eagerly, their small tools clinking against the ice as they chattered like a gathering of squirrels stashing away nuts.

Amber strolled beside him toward the next workstation, a satisfied grin on her face.

"I didn't know you knew how to do that," Cooper admitted.

She glanced up. "I have many talents."

"*That* I already knew. And thank goodness for them." His tone was dry yet slightly teasing, and her face lit up in a way that sent a thrill through him.

Dammit, this was so unfair. He *wanted* to do things that made Amber happy. He wanted to put that kind of expression on her face every single day, but he couldn't. Not yet.

They kept walking, Amber stepping carefully over the uneven ground, her boots sinking into the powdery snow. "I went to a number of ice-carving events with one of my foster families. Mom was a decent artist and always interested in trying new things. Mason and I learned alongside her."

"Mason. Your brother?" He'd heard parts of this story, but it was good to get extra details.

Amber nodded, but before she could say anything else, they were called to help a group of four who were creating an Inuksuk from their block of ice. The man-shaped structure had tipped slightly when one of them accidentally removed too large of a chunk from one side.

Cooper reached out a hand to help balance the massive ice block as Amber darted forward, and he ended up with his arms on either side of her body.

She was pinned under him, pressed against the ice. Pressed against his front. He eased off instantly, trying to move away from her, but a loud crack sounded, and another section of ice fell away.

The entire sculpture leaned precariously toward them, a second away from toppling and crushing them both under its massive weight.

4

---

*A*mber had dreamed of being pinned under Cooper's sexy body far too many times, but to be perfectly honest, her fantasies had never involved a giant block of ice.

A second later, the arms on either side of her flexed and an urgent command rumbled. "As soon as there's room, duck away."

With a Herculean effort from Cooper, the block of ice tilted back toward vertical, the pressure easing enough that she could dart to safety, twirling to check no one else was in the danger zone.

More people had rushed over to help, and in the end, the ice was placed firmly and safely on the ground.

"There goes that idea," one of the teenagers complained, kicking his toe against the unrecognizable sculpture.

"We'll figure something else out," the girl at his side encouraged, slapping him on the back and quickly pointing out other options.

Amber and Cooper watched for a moment, but it was

clear they weren't needed anymore. Instead, she twisted toward the big bear shifter, looking him over carefully to make sure he hadn't been hurt.

She dusted off a layer of powdery ice that clung to his arm. "Thank you for making sure I didn't get crushed."

"Didn't think this activity was going to be that dangerous," Cooper admitted. "Except for the knives—those I knew could be trouble."

"And the chainsaws. But don't worry, I'm fully capable of using those as well." She glanced around the field to see if anybody was trying to catch their attention. "The only thing I don't seem capable of is juggling massive ice cubes."

"I promise to do all the ice cube juggling necessary," Cooper told her with a laugh. "Tell me more about your foster mom. I assume that's who taught you to use a chainsaw as well as an electric knife."

"Her and our dad. They were the best family we ever got placed with. Mason and I were five and six when our birth parents died. We were already in our teens and had gone through a dozen placements when the Jordans got us. That's the stage when most kids in the system only live with their foster families for a brief time then leave as soon as they age out. The Jordans were different. They really wanted us, and daily living turned out to be an education all in itself." She followed him to one of the benches that had been placed center field so they could easily observe the action. "We lived in a pretty remote cabin in northern Ontario, and everything was off-grid and homegrown."

Cooper's big blue eyes danced with curiosity as he examined her. "I didn't know that."

She shrugged. "I don't talk about them a lot. Kaylee knows the story, but it was pretty much just Mason and me for as long as I could remember. The Jordans were amazing after a long line of not-so-spectacular placements. They were the closest thing to a family we ever had. They went missing about four years ago when their ultralight went down somewhere in the north."

Sudden understanding lit Cooper's expression. "*That's* why your brother came north a couple of years ago. He was trying to find out what happened to them."

Amber nodded. "Their downed aircraft was found, but there was no sign of either of my parents. The fact Mason later vanished as well made everything harder."

Someone called at that moment, and Cooper rose, reaching back to help Amber to her feet.

The moment of contact felt so very real. Warm and connected. It was an illusion, though. Amber knew that to her core. No matter how much she admired the big bear, she wasn't going to ignore the truth when it came to their relationship.

Being with him today, having him listen to her as a friend instead of an employee—it was only the start and not the end point she was aiming at.

But simply getting to spend time with him right now had to be a priority.

She glanced across the field to where James was chasing Kaylee across the snow before they tumbled to the ground in each other's arms.

Lara stood with an ever-present group of wolves at her side, the ones who needed to stick close to their Alpha to feel safe. Alex was a short distance away, helping Dixon and a group of teenage boys lift a large triangle onto a round platform. But even as he worked with the others, Alex's gaze slipped back to Lara, and they exchanged a wink and a smile that made Amber's heart pound hard.

Mates. *Fated* mates, and they'd found each other this

year because the patriarch of Borealis Gems had forced their hands. The boys hadn't even tried to keep the mating-fever pact a secret from their mates, and what Kaylee and Lara knew, Amber knew.

She glanced at Cooper. She'd bet everything that he had some trick up his sleeve to deal with the ultimatum, but what if...

What if he gave in to the mating fever with another woman? Forget the fact that him getting physical with someone else would make her furious, what if that week of togetherness became the start of a real relationship, like it had for Alex and Lara?

Amber didn't want to watch him fall in love with someone else. Not because she didn't want him to be happy, but because she was sure that *she* could make him happy.

Cooper and Amber paced across the field toward where Alex had waved an arm to get their attention. "I wonder what insults he's dreamed up in the past thirty minutes?" Cooper drawled.

Amber snorted. "Your brother is competitive."

"So am I," Cooper said mildly. "Only I don't feel the need to announce my superiority at every turn."

"Naturally. Those who have it don't need to flaunt it."

A burst of laughter rang from him. The others glanced their way, but Cooper ignored them, smiling down at her with approval and amusement.

Amber returned his smile.

He was a good man, and while things might be advancing slower than she'd like, she was more determined than ever to make this happen. She knew his methods. She knew how his brain worked, and now she just needed to be ready when it was time to make her move.

They stopped near a project that was progressing

nicely. The huge shape that had been lifted into place earlier was a slice of pizza, of all things, resting on a raised serving platter. The entire sculpture was tilted slightly to the side so the surface could be admired.

Slices with pepperoni and olives stuck up from the background, but as Amber slid into position next to Kaylee, she found herself distracted. The team had made the cheese seem to drip off the edge of the one piece near the edge of the platter, and...

Oh no.

Giggles threatened to set in and knock her off her feet.

She leaned toward Kaylee. "There's... Am I seeing what I think I'm seeing?"

A snicker escaped her best friend. "Maybe?"

"Oh my goodness," Amber whispered as she stared at the long, contoured drips.

On her other side, Lara joined them. She rested her head on Amber's shoulder and all but whimpered as if in agony. "I can't say anything. I need to say something, but I just can't..."

She broke off into hysterical hiccups.

Alex glanced over, alarm rising. He paced around the gathering toward them, James moving quickly as well.

"Are they using the mate connection in your heads to ask why we're snickering?" Amber got out between sputters. "Because, oh dear, you can't tell them. But you *have* to tell them."

"Can't. *You* deal with this," Kaylee told Lara as firmly as she could before grabbing hold of James and burying her face against his chest so she could cover up her squall of laughter.

Lara pulled herself vertical, took one look at the pizza,

then turned back to Amber before collapsing to the ground, clutching her stomach as she gasped for air.

Cooper had joined them now, a frown creasing his face as he took in the situation. "Amber?"

She sealed her lips together and shook her head frantically. He stood between her and the ice sculpture, and one of the thick, dripping icicles was visible behind his shoulder.

Amber closed her eyes and prayed for strength.

Cooper's soft touch on her shoulder and the warmth of his breath over her face calmed her slightly, but her cheeks were still flaming hot as he spoke softly.

"They put rabbit parts on the pizza, didn't they?" he asked.

Amber jerked upright, thankful for a good solution that didn't involve describing the real issue. "A Bunny Special? Well..."

She glanced at the pizza. Turns out the team, aided and abetted by Dixon from the Orion wolf pack *had* carved what appeared to be a few sets of bunny ears on the surface. But as she looked over the group, she realized she couldn't let it go without mentioning what had set her and her friends off.

Amber caught Cooper by the front of the shirt and tugged him close enough so she could whisper in his ear. "The cheese that's dripping off. It looks less like cheese and more like...other things. Things that's shouldn't be hanging out in a public gathering."

Cooper stayed close but tilted his head to the side to take a peek. "I see them. Drips. I don't know what—"

"Penises. Many penis. Penii? Cooper, every one of those drips is X-rated."

He froze. Blinked.

Her cheeks flared hotter as his gaze drifted over the half dozen tube-shaped objects. Melting had caused water to run down toward the bottom of each drip where it had cooled and gathered to create a wider "head." Veins and ridges were there as well, and if it weren't so terrible, it would be astonishing how lifelike they were.

Lifelike and very impressive. Ahem.

Cooper cleared his throat. "Oh. *Oh*, I see."

So dignified. So mature.

Until he threw back his head and howled with laughter. Which set off Amber and her friends again.

It took a bit until he got himself under control, and his smile was still wide when he offered her a wink. "I'll deal with this. If you see a chance to fix things, take it."

She sort of pulled herself together. "Sure."

Alex had managed to pull Lara to her feet but had yet to get a straight answer out of her about why they were laughing.

Cooper called to his brother. "Nice job, bro. You might want to help the team check the base over here, though. Looks as if there's a fault line developing."

"Where?" Alex left Lara's side and moved toward Cooper quickly.

Amber might have imagined it, but it looked as if Lara shot out a foot and suddenly Alex was flying through the air, his feet slipping out from under him. He was aimed straight at the ice sculpture and disaster seemed imminent.

Cooper caught hold of his sleeve and tugged, changing his direction in midflight. Instead of wiping out the entire piece of pizza, Alex's head neatly grazed the long line of drips, sending the erotically shaped objects crashing to the ground where most of them shattered into non-pornographic ice cubes.

Amber slipped nonchalantly toward the few intact ones and cautiously kicked them aside into the snow. Disaster averted.

"You make a good team," Kaylee said as the bell rang to signal the end of the contest.

"I had no idea what was going on until Kaylee told me." James wore a slight smirk as he cuddled his mate close. "Too bad all of them got broken."

"James." Kaylee sounded shocked.

Amber twisted her face downward to hide her burning cheeks, but she grinned as well. There had been something more than amusement in Cooper's eyes. There'd been desire.

Desire for her.

Yes, as the afternoon progressed and she shared time with the Borealis family, Amber felt a strange sense of contentment fall over her. It wasn't going to be simple, but she knew enough to make her move at the right time.

And the right time was going to be when Cooper most needed her to be there for him.

Whether he put it in his Very Important Plans list, or not.

5

The dull itch at the back of his neck was growing stronger by the day.

Cooper had ignored the sensation for nearly a week before acknowledging what it was. The mating fever was close to arriving, and he was running out of time.

His desk chair was angled perfectly so that with his office door open, a mirrorlike reflection appeared in the inset glass. Every time Amber walked from the filing cabinet and back to her desk, Cooper got an unhindered view of the journey. She'd move decisively, disappear for a moment, then return and sit.

Then she'd cross her legs and, a few moments later, uncross them—

One day the uncrossing was going to kill him.

It wasn't fair. It wasn't right. Both the part where he was ogling an employee and the fact that mere legs shouldn't send his orderly, controlled world into chaos.

I bet she's got cute toes.

You're not helping matters, Cooper told his bear bluntly. *You're moving too slow, and you're useless when you're this distracted,* the beast retorted. *Perhaps you need to do a little more thinking about her toes and the rest of her. Naked toes. Naked her.*

Do you mind? Cooper snapped, hideously disappointed with himself as a vivid image of Amber sans clothing appeared in his brain. *We've gone over why the logical reason is to wait for at least another year.*

Yada, yada, yada. His bear snarled the words. *Logic, schmogic.*

Thank goodness Cooper had a huge distraction waiting for him at the end of the day. Amber had taken off before he was done. He closed down the office then headed straight over to his grandparents' home.

He left his car at the side of the driveway and slipped into the cool comfort of the massive log building. Polished wooden floors were warm underfoot, and the air carried the sound of voices along with delicate music and the scent of his grandmother's cooking. A homey, comfortable sensation to stave off all the other conflicting emotions.

"Good to see you, bro." James offered him a firm pat on the back followed quickly by a hefty glass of scotch. He eyed Cooper. "Good thing it's nearly the holidays. You're looking a little tired."

"Year-end is always busy," Cooper offered as an excuse. He slipped over to where his grandmother was stirring something at the stove and pressed a kiss to her cheek. "Your invitation to dinner was unexpected, but as usual, it smells like a million dollars in here."

"I don't think I can get quite that much for my gravy, but thanks, sweetheart." Grandmother Laureen adjusted her position so she could press her hand against his cheek. "You're working too hard. You should plan a bit of a getaway soon. Give yourself a chance to refresh and get your feet under you."

Considering the warning signs were there for the arrival of mating fever, having her offer an excuse to make himself scarce in the coming days was exactly what he was looking for. "I think I might just do that. But I'll definitely be around for the family holiday events."

Kaylee and Lara dodged past to grab plates and set the table for dinner.

Grandmother waved a hand at him. "Of course I *want* to see you all here for Christmas, but only if it works out. Sometimes the best laid plans have to be put aside when something else comes up."

He eyed her closely. The comment about plans hit a little too close to home, but she wasn't even looking at him. Instead she gave a final stir to whatever was in the pot before tossing orders at his brothers and sisters-in-law. They each came to claim a heavily laden bowl to set on the table.

Grandmother Laureen whirled on Alex, pointing to a platter heaped high with steaks. "Those to the table, please. I'll bring the buns, and that will be everything. Oh, and Cooper, please be a darling and track down your grandfather. I have no idea where he's gotten to."

Cooper headed out in search of the family patriarch. The old man wasn't that hard to find, his deep chuckle echoing from near the front door.

"Grandfather. It's time for dinner—"

Cooper rounded the corner and stumbled to a stop. Grandfather was helping Amber out of her coat.

She twisted toward him and offered a shy smile.

Oh baby, his bear rumbled happily.

Stop that. You're so annoying.

She looks delicious.

40

What part of stop *don't you understand?*

The part where I think you want to lick her from the bottom of her toes to the tip of her—

His grandfather interrupted his childish mental chatter, an impossibly serious expression on his face as he motioned to Cooper. "She's such a delight. Why, I just barely mentioned to Amber I hoped I could read over those year-end reports, and look. She's here with them. I think she should join us for dinner."

"Oh no." Amber blinked then stuttered briefly. "I mean, *yes*, I did bring the reports, but I thought I had been invited..."

She trailed off, obviously embarrassed.

Cooper stepped forward quickly to reassure her. "Grandfather's right. You should stay. There's plenty from what I just saw—Grandmother cooks enough for an army of bears, and I know the girls would love to visit with you."

She blinked before lifting her gaze to meet his firmly. "Thank you. It's very kind of you all to welcome me."

Grandfather had vanished—probably hightailing it out of sight before Cooper could give him the evil eye.

It wasn't the best timing, not with the fever so close, but there was no way he wanted Amber to feel awkward when soon enough she would be a part of this family. *Soon* being a relative term.

Cooper wasn't going to allow his grandfather's misguided, cheery "you're part of the gang" attitude to interfere with the eventual wooing of said maiden.

As expected, the rest of the family was thrilled when Cooper and Amber entered the room.

"Amber. Come sit beside me," Kaylee ordered, hurrying to the kitchen to grab another place setting. She bounced down one chair from where she'd been, opening up a space for her friend. Which meant Amber settled across from Lara with Cooper on her other side.

"Thanks for letting me interrupt your family time," Amber said as Cooper pushed in her chair.

Grandmother waved off the comment. "It's not an official family meal. I had a bunch of recipes that needed to be tested, and the next thing I knew, Kaylee and I had cooked enough to feed an army. And my favourite portable army is on speed dial."

Conversation passed around the table with the heaping platters of food. Comfortable. Easy.

"Hey, Amber. Needed to tell you. One of the pack who's out on an extended trip said he heard rumours about your brother's whereabouts. It's in a village that's not satellite accessible, so we can't call them to find out. He's double-checking before he sends anyone on a wild goose chase." Lara's voice was filled with excitement. "But he told me he was pretty sure it was Mason they were talking about."

"I thought you weren't going to say anything until you were positive." Alex's words were soft but still chiding.

Beside Cooper, Amber snapped upright.

"I need to know, and I *want* to know, even if it's not one hundred percent sure. Just hearing a little bit gives me hope," she insisted, staring Alex down intently as if his shifter form weren't a predator more than twice her size.

His lips twitched, then he tilted his head toward his mate. "You've got a fierce protector there, sugar. Nice to know the human in the room has your back."

"*One* of the humans in the room," his grandmother noted in passing before smiling at Amber approvingly. "And this human agrees. It's worth hearing all the threads in the hopes one of them can be tugged to find the right trail."

"I'll be sure to let you know as soon as I hear more," Lara promised. She glanced around the table and shared with a grin, "Other than that, the pack is wild these days while they wait for Christmas. You'd think we had a dozen or more kids in the pack house from the carrying on."

"What will you do once you have kids?" Amber asked before slapping a hand over her mouth. "Oops. Rude human question. I'm sorry. I wasn't asking about you and Alex having kids, because that's totally up to you when you have them. Or *if* you have them. I don't want to presume..." Her face scrunched up before she offered a wan smile. "If I open my mouth wider, I might be able to fit both feet in there."

Lara laughed. "I know what you were asking in the first place. The logistics of wolf-pack living arrangements *are* entertaining. The pack house is for adults, and anyone living there who has kids usually moves into a single-family dwelling nearby. Only as Alphas, Alex and I will stay at the house. We'll add more rooms to our apartment based on how many kids we end up with."

James glanced at Kaylee, who smiled as he spoke up. "We want kids, but down the road a bit."

Alex was nodding his agreement, going shell-shocked when Lara said, "Oh, I'd like them as soon as possible."

"Kids? Right away?" Alex swallowed then smiled, his expression a little shaky around the edges. "Really?"

"Definitely. If we're going to have a nice, big family, we'd better get started on it soon. You've got three kids in your family, I've got five...maybe we should split the difference."

James grinned evilly as Alex struggled to stay on an even keel. "Or you could go for a record. Six. Or seven would be cool."

"*Seven?*" Alex choked on the word, but he forced his lips into a tormented smile. "We can discuss this later, sugar."

"Of course, sweetie." Lara winked at Amber then grabbed the bowl in front of her and passed it to one side.

The conversation shifted to other topics as plates were refilled and glasses topped up. Cooper found sitting next to Amber a form of sweet torture. Their legs brushed every now and then, and in spite of the turkey and braised brussels sprouts and roast salmon and everything else at the table, the scent of her was the strongest thing in the room.

Still, it wasn't until he noticed the wine seemed off that he excused himself from the table. Standing in the bathroom, Cooper flipped quickly through his notes. Sure enough, on the Signs Of Impending Mating Fever page was the kicker: *liquor tastes bad.*

It was time to take measures.

Cooper opened the booking for the remote wilderness cabin reservation he'd begun a few weeks earlier. He clicked the confirmation then returned to the table with a sense of peace.

Everything was under control.

Or at least it was until he got ready to leave the house and discovered he and Amber were the only ones left. His brothers had been eager to get alone with their mates, and his grandfather had vanished off somewhere.

But there Amber was, pulling on her coat as his grandmother spoke with her.

Grandmother Laureen reached out and patted Amber's hand. "Thanks for staying and explaining that to me, dear. Cooper will walk you to your car."

"I'm okay on my own, Mrs. Borealis."

"Nonsense." His grandmother's eyes flashed brightly.

"What's the use of having fine, strapping grandsons if I can't commandeer them to do my bidding every now and then?"

She closed the door behind them, and silence fell. It had begun to snow, and the teeny crystals tumbled around them like icing sugar.

"Come on." Cooper offered his arm and waited until Amber wrapped her gloved hand around his bicep. The distance to her vehicle was both too short and far too long considering his bear spent the duration all but screaming at him to pick her up and go find a cave.

They'd just stopped by her car when she turned decisively, took a deep breath, and spoke. "Come to my place for drink. It's early still, and I'd love to spend some time with you outside the office."

From the look in her eyes to the way she stood, it was crystal clear Amber was offering him every green light he'd ever dreamed of. It was unexpected—he'd hoped she'd be amiable to his courting in a few years, but this was out of the blue and Not On The Agenda.

And then she caught him even more off guard. She slid a hand up and around his neck, tugging him toward her. Close enough that when she lifted her face, it was her lips and his lips, with no space between them.

A kiss out of time. It wasn't supposed to happen, but it was happening, and as her lips ghosted over his, he would have sworn that a million light bulbs went on around them and lit the darkness with a neon glow.

Cooper pulled back slightly. He was towering over her, but the look in her eyes said she was meeting him straight on. Equal to equal, not just in desire but in decision. God, he wanted that to be true, but there were still multiple items on his list that needed to be dealt with before they could do anything permanent.

So do something temporary, his bear suggested.

Busy, Cooper warned the beast.

Doesn't look like it to me, his inner animal complained.

"Cooper?" Amber slid her hand along his jawline, then up to his hair, where she brushed it back, fingers tugging slightly. Her touch sizzled, wrapping around his body like a great big Christmas bow and tying him up firmly. Need raced upward, boiling and bubbling.

Her fingers tightened and she pulled him toward her again, and damn it if he wasn't moving with her.

Now it wasn't her encouragement that made him change position, but his need to possess and take and touch. He kissed her willing lips, drinking deeply from the sweetness of her mouth, and the thrill of brightness accompanying the contact made it all too clear how perfect things were going to be—when it was time.

Which wasn't now, damn it all.

He pushed away all of the annoying thoughts about time and place and having to wait, and instead focused on what he had to enjoy right now. Her mouth on his, her hands clutching his shoulders as she leaned toward him. Thick layers of coat separated them, and yet he could feel her arching hard to press them closer.

Her tongue slipped along his, and a noise of pleasure rumbled from his chest to mix with her purr of need.

When he finally managed to break the kiss, her lips were swollen, her eyes bright. She breathed hard, cheeks flushed with excitement.

Then he did the hardest thing he'd ever had to do. He let go, peeling his fingers off her hips and forcing his feet backward until the separation between them was a good two feet—three feet—four feet and increasing.

He exhaled hard but met her eyes. "I'll see you in a few days. We'll talk then."

"But Cooper—"

He ignored the longing in her voice, turned on his heel, and walked away. He was either the smartest bear in the world or he'd just thrown away everything he needed for his future happiness.

Following through on his This Needs To Be Done Right Now list sucked.

6

*I*t took a moment for the initial shock to fade.

He'd kissed her, damn it. That hadn't simply been her pushing herself on him. Although he hadn't expected it, Cooper had been 100 percent on board with the intimate contact.

How could he walk away?

Amber cursed a few times, but there was a cold wind whipping around her, so she slipped into her car and slammed the door shut. Getting frostbite wasn't going to help her whoop Cooper's ass.

His ass totally needed whooping.

She closed her eyes as she pressed back against the headrest, hoping the solid connection would stop the spinning. Fever-pitch desire burned, and she wasn't sure what was going on.

She hadn't meant to kiss him. Asking him to come over had been a bold move on her part, egged on slightly by how well she thought things had gone during dinner and a few chance comments during her talk with Laureen Borealis.

The woman had said something about living without

48

regrets and seizing the moment, and there'd been a fire in the words that had fanned the coals inside Amber and pushed her to act.

And he'd kissed her back, *dammit*.

So why...?

She drove the short distance home so she wasn't sitting outside the Borealis homestead. The last thing she needed was for Giles or Laureen to spot her sitting there in a daze and come out to see what was wrong.

As she made her way up the stairs to her apartment, Amber's phone buzzed. She checked it without thinking, mindlessly staring at the calendar update that had arrived.

Booking confirmation: Cabin In The Woods motel. 1 occupant, 7 nights. Special instructions followed and in place. Please let us know if you need anything else during your stay.

Amber blinked, read it again, then opened it to see if there was any more information because she truly was confused. When she realized the alert was from the work calendar linked between her and Cooper, and he had booked himself into a remote retreat house for a week starting the next day, everything became clear in a rush.

He hadn't walked away from her because he didn't want her. Cooper was trying to protect her.

She didn't need protecting. She needed *him*.

Amber took a deep breath. Also, he needed *her*.

She checked the reservation again, but it was for one person. He wasn't taking off to some love nest without anyone being the wiser, but the week away clearly indicated a major event.

Something big, like the arrival of mating fever.

It made sense. Right now, with the holidays approaching and more than a few to-do items still on his list? Cooper wasn't the type to up and leave his responsibilities without planning ahead.

She thought she'd been brave to ask him over, but it seemed that was only the tip of the iceberg of exactly how daring she needed to be. Amber headed into her apartment and pulled out a suitcase even as she made plans of her own.

Out of consideration for her friends, she waited until the following morning to start a text conversation.

Amber: *Question for one or both of you*

Lara: *I'm up. What's happening?*

Amber paused in the middle of typing her question because ...*what do you suggest as the best way to seduce Cooper*... came off as far creepier than intended.

She must have paused for too long because she got back an exasperated comment.

Lara: *I will kick your behind into tomorrow if you woke me up early to rewrite messages at me*

Amber: *Fine. Bluntly speaking, Cooper is going into the mating fever, and I intend to join him. Do you have any suggestions since I'm human and not sure what to expect?*

Lara: ...

Lara: ...

Lara: ...

Amber rolled her eyes. Okay, now she understood how totally annoying it was to have someone write and erase messages. She wanted information, stat. She had places to drive to and a bear to get naked with.

Oh dear, she was going after a polar bear headed into mating fever, and they would end up having sex, and she was a human, and what was she thinking, but this was exactly what she wanted.

Amber: *Say something before I freak out. Do you think this is a terrible idea?*

Lara: *Sorry about that. I screamed when I read your message, and then I had to wrestle Alex to get my phone back before he could see what you wrote.*

Amber rested her forehead on the table in front of her. Great. She hadn't even made it to Cooper's hideout, hadn't even had a chance to be rejected, and his brothers were going to know what she was up to.

It was one thing to have her friends know. It was another entirely for the whole family to be aware.

Kaylee joined the conversation then, her online button turning green a second before she dropped into the conversation.

Kaylee: *OH. EM. GEE. Are you serious, Amber?*

Lara: *Of course she's serious. They've had the hots for each other for ages. It's been very...ahem...aromatically apparent.*

Amber: *I hate your wolf nose. Just saying.*

Lara: *I've been polite and never mentioned it! Very polite, even though sometimes I'd swear...never mind. Suffice to say, I've noticed.*

Amber: *Can we get back to the question at hand? If you don't think me going to Cooper is a terrible idea, am I still stepping over a line? I need you guys to help me here, because if you tell me I should stay away, I will.*

Kaylee: *Bluntly speaking: you know this could end up with you two the equivalent of married? It could be a lot more than simply a week-long fling.*

Amber: *Understood. I'm truly okay with that.*

Lara: *There's a brave human.*

Amber: *Brave or reckless. You tell me.*

Kaylee and Lara both started messages at the same time. They both posted at the same instant, and a second later, Amber's eyes filled with moisture. Her girlfriends were the best.

Kaylee: *Recklessly brave, because you know taking a chance is worth it. I'm so glad James took a chance on me because he really is my everything.*

Lara: *Brave enough to be willing to be reckless because it's what you want and what you think is right. Like Alex with me—we truly belonged together, but he took the chance and made it happen.*

This was why they were her best friends, and she was so thankful to have them in her world.

Amber: *I love you guys.*

Kaylee: *Love you too. So, the mating fever thing? If he's in it, be ready to get very, very sexed.*

Lara: *Bluntly speaking. Don't mention other men, don't mention leaving him, not even to get some privacy.*

Kaylee: *The leaving thing—yeah, he's going to be stuck like glue within touching range all week. Don't waste room in your suitcase for clothes. Pack energy bars.*

Lara: *Good point. And chafing power. And KY jelly. And drink lots so you can pee after every bout of sex to avoid getting a UTI.*

Kaylee and Lara alternated with sexual suggestions for another five minutes. Amber's face was burning hot, but she took mental notes the entire time before finally posting again.

Amber: *Now I will pretend this conversation never happened, and I expect you two to do the same. Cone of silence, especially with your guys, at least for the week, okay? And Kaylee, can you cover for me at work? I went in and did everything time-sensitive last night and made a schedule for you to follow.*

Kaylee: *No problem!*

Lara: I won't say a word. I might have to duct tape Alex to something to stop him from hacking into my phone to read these messages, though. But you know, that could be fun…
Amber:*I'll be in touch. Thanks for everything.*

It was a short enough drive to the cabin that second-guessing didn't have a chance to set in. Amber stopped at the main office before inching her way down a long bumpy road to where the teeny cabin sat on its own at the edge of a wide, north-facing clearing.

It was a pristine location, where the clean white snow spread out like a wedding dress. She parked beside Cooper's truck, took a deep breath and headed to the porch.

The key she'd gotten from the host turned smoothly in the lock, and a moment later she'd slipped inside the woodsmoke-scented space. The curtains were pulled back, and sunshine fell across the wooden floor in wide bands. Oddly, a shiny silver chain looped like a snake back and forth across the floor's surface, but the bed was where her attention settled.

Cooper was stretched out on the home-style quilt, breathing heavily. His chest heaved as if he'd just finished a race. His face was folded in a grimace, pain drifting over his features.

Something inside Amber broke. If nothing else came of this week other than her easing that pain, it would be worth it.

She slipped off her shoes and removed her coat. She wasn't particularly quiet, although she didn't speak. Still, Cooper lay oblivious to her presence.

Alrighty then. Time to go big since she wasn't going home.

Amber laid a hand on the mattress and stared down at him. "Cooper?"

No answer. Just a low moan of pain.

The sound wrenched her heart tighter, and she couldn't bear it. "Cooper. I'm here. It's going to be okay."

Another moan, and Amber broke. She crawled on the edge of the bed so she could lean over him. She stroked his face, then knelt beside him to balance better. "Cooper. Open your eyes. It's me, Amber."

His hands rose to her hips. Big strong hands that grabbed her tight before one eased up her back, applying pressure until she leaned over him. Closer. Closer.

Amber pressed her hands to his chest. She whispered softly, hoping to break though whatever cage he'd built around himself. "It's okay, Cooper. I'm here for you. Whatever you need, I promise I'm ready for it."

His eyes opened, and it was the bear staring at her.

t couldn't be real. Cooper swallowed hard and decided the fact he was currently daydreaming about the woman he wanted with a deep obsession had to be some weird trick of the mating fever that kicked in once a man passed thirty-five.

"No." The word escaped in a rush. "You're not really here. You *can't* be here. Imaginary-you needs to leave, right now."

Amber tilted her head to one side. Considered. Shook it in denial. "Can't."

Cooper curled himself upright, cursing inwardly as that brought him right against her soft curves. His hands shook as he lifted them, planning to physically grab her and lift her away. Time was ticking.

Hmmmmmmmm.

Yeah. The arrival of his bear was part of what he was worried about.

Don't do anything. Don't think *anything,* Cooper warned.

It was too late. A flood of desire raced through him,

initiated by his bear half. Dirty images of what should happen next arrived in high-speed, high definition—and the thought of rolling Amber under him, stripping her naked, and licking her was the tamest of them.

The chain attached to his wrist clicked, and her brows rose higher. "Cooper. What have you done?"

"Was taking care of business." Speaking was tough and getting tougher because all the blood in his body had pooled in the section of his anatomy centered under her hips.

Amber caught his wrist in her hand and lifted, examining the heavy cuff. "Isn't this a little over-the-top and, at the same time, useless? If the idea was to lock yourself away for a week, great. Only your bear could break this in an instant."

What a brilliant idea. One that in his current state of Racing Toward The Edge Of Desperation, he'd never have come up with on his own.

He'd deliberately come to this place to avoid seeking Amber out before it was appropriate. At the same time, he'd promised to honour the pledge he'd made with his brothers. That meant no shifting to escape this mating fever.

But if it came to a choice between them and Amber, she won every time. Alex and James would more than understand, considering the situation.

Only, when Cooper tried to change into his bear form, nothing happened. He still felt Amber's weight resting on his very human anatomy, and dear Lord, in a minute he was going to do something they'd both regret.

We need to shift, he told his bear.

A leisurely sort of shrug was followed instantly by another round of dirty images, this time accompanied by an internal evil laugh.

What is wrong with you? Cooper demanded. *Help me. We need to shift. Now.*

Oh, we definitely don't. You see, you made me promise. "No shifting and breaking out of this room. I need to stay human, and so no matter how much I beg, promise we'll stay human for the duration of this fever." Sound familiar? You said it ad nauseam, so I can repeat it if necessary.

Cooper's heart sank. *Oh. Right. That.*

Yeah. That. His bear did the equivalent of a cocky "I told you so" shrug before going more serious. Almost sad, in some strange way. *I need to go dark. Have fun, and I'll see you in a week.*

Before he could protest, his other half was gone. Vanished to wherever the beast went when Cooper was in charge.

As awareness returned, he refocused his gaze to discover Amber held him, her palms pressed to his face. "Cooper? Are you talking to yourself?"

"Yeah," he admitted. "Oh, Amber. What have you done?"

She looked thoughtful. "I came because you needed me."

Hopefulness skyrocketed, but he held on to his control. "I've got the mating fever. You know what will happen if you stay?"

She nodded, but her eyes were wide. The pulse at the base of her throat throbbed, and a shiver rolled over her.

Dammit. She was scared. He was scaring her, and that wasn't acceptable.

Before he could find the strength to comfort her and tell her everything would be okay—a.k.a., lie his ass off—Amber brushed her knuckles over his cheek and simultaneously knocked him senseless.

"If you don't want me, just say that and I'll leave right now. I don't want to make you do anything you don't want, Cooper."

He gaped at her. "I don't want...?"

She stilled.

Shit. Oh, hell no. Bad timing for him to be stuttering out half phrases.

Cooper rolled. Levitated, possibly. Because when they landed on the mattress again, she was under him, trapped in place by his vastly bigger torso. "Let me say that properly. I want you. I have for a long time."

"Me too. Want you," Amber confessed before continuing in a firm clear voice. "I want this. I want you, Cooper. Whatever we need to figure out, we'll deal with at a better time."

Then she tangled her hands behind his neck and tugged.

Screw the lists and charts and all the long-term plans in the world. Mating fever was on him, he had a willing partner, and for the first time in his life, he was going to enjoy the hell out of this week.

A fan-fucking-tastic place to begin was by kissing the woman he planned to enjoy from now to eternity.

Cooper leaned closer and let nature take control. In this case, that meant lips connecting as a searing heat flashed through his entire body. As if her mouth meeting his was the final circuit that allowed the full charge of desire to let loose and race at high speed through his system.

He all but inhaled her. Soft lips, tongues touching, a sigh of pleasure. Taste and sound blended together. They were only beginning, and it was already the best sexual experience of his life.

Amber pushed at his shirt, and he shrugged when

prompted to ease the fabric off his shoulders. The entire time he kept kissing her because her mouth was temptation and ambrosia and seriously addictive.

When her hands hit his bare skin, another electric rush struck. Desire was a heavy weight in his gut, but her soft sound of approval as she scraped her nails over his skin was a heavenly chorus.

Cooper left her mouth for a moment, nibbling and sucking his way along her jaw to under her ear. "You taste like sunshine. Sunshine and hot, sweaty sex."

A soft laugh escaped her. "Thank you? I think?"

"Oh, it's a good thing. Trust me." Cooper leaned on an elbow and went for her buttons, wrenching to a stop when the chain around his wrist clanked against the handcuff. "Dammit."

Amber giggled this time, squirming upright. "Where's the key?"

"I don't know."

She paused. "Really?"

Seriously bad planning on his part, that was for sure. "I stole them from Alex. I was going to message him to come set me free when the fever was done."

Her eyes lit up. "Very well thought out plan. Now, hold still." A few seconds later she'd popped the cuff free from his wrist and was undoing her buttons. "You can thank Lara later for telling me the secret to opening these without a key."

Cooper would worry about his brothers, their mates, and what the hell was going on with their sex lives at some other time. His hunger was growing by the second. As an older bear, his control was good, but even he had a breaking point.

The final straw was seeing Amber slip out of her blouse

and stand before him, her beautiful brown skin highlighted by a pale pink bra. He picked her up, kicked the chain away without a thought, and carried her back to bed.

Warm skin brushed his cheek a second before Cooper gave in to all his fantasies and began.

Sucking. Biting. Kissing.

He worked his way along the edge of her bra then tipped back the cup and took a long, leisurely lick over the top of her breast.

Yum.

He tugged back the fabric a little more, his finger caught the top of the cup so he could slowly reveal her delicious reddish-brown nipple.

Amber arched under him, lifting up toward his mouth as he pulled the taut peak between his lips and sucked. Softly, then harder. Nibbling now, the bra completely pushed aside so he could access the entire mound.

She moaned and tangled her fingers in his hair. Holding him close as he played and teased. It was the start to fulfilling every fantasy he'd had. A gasp escaped her as he rolled his thumbs and forefingers together over both nipples at the same time.

"God, you're beautiful."

Amber glanced at him from under hooded lashes, but he was already moving to lick and suck the hard tips again. And again. And again, just because he could.

Cooper slid a hand under her torso and lifted her toward him, speeding up his teasing. One breast got a nip and a suck, then the other. His free hand cupped her firmly, the heated sweep of her filling his hand. She was delicious... with more to enjoy.

Oh, yes. There were other delicious places to go, the scent in the air reminded him.

He dropped her to the mattress and grabbed hold of her pants. A moment later he had her naked from the waist down.

"Cooper." His name was a sharp cry on her lips. He wanted to hear it as a plea. As a call of praise. As a benediction.

But first, he reluctantly left the sweetness of her nipples for a slow exploration down her body. Kisses to the underside of her breasts. A nip at her waist. A stop to stab his tongue into her bellybutton, which drew a burst of laughter from her.

But the entire time he kept licking. Tasting. Teasing.

Cooper pushed her legs apart and settled between them, preparing to stay a while.

Amber lifted up on her elbows. Her bra was tangled around her rib cage, and her body was flushed with heat. Her eyes glittered with passion.

He nipped her inner thigh, and she gasped.

Oh, yeah. He'd get more of those noises from her. He needed to hear them. Needed her.

Cooper lowered his head and buried his mouth against her sex.

8

*S*he'd been warned.

There was no one she could complain to because she'd been *warned*, but dealing with Cooper in the throes of mating fever was going to make sexual saturation a reality.

The intensity of the situation made the slightest touch more erotic. He'd been surprisingly silent since their clothes had begun to come off, but Amber didn't mind one bit.

He was saying with body language everything that needed to be said.

The pressure of his tongue on her sex and clit stayed focused. A near brutal demand that her body answer the call to pleasure, and her body responded with a "hey, howdy, and hello" that would have thrilled any porn shoot director.

She'd wondered for a moment if it was possible to orgasm from the nipple play alone.

Amber had no doubts that a record-breaking climax was rising as Cooper upped his game and turned his tongue and fingers into a sexual torture device.

Just enough licking on her clit to make tingles start along her spine. Barely enough play with his oversized finger at the opening of her sex. Another round, literally, with his tongue. He started a slide in then out with his finger on slow-motion repeat until she was perched on top of a rocket with a burning fuse and an impending explosion.

Everything stopped.

Amber's head snapped off the mattress and she growled at him. "*Cooper.*"

An amused and evil grin twisted his lips. "Just making sure you're paying attention."

She didn't have time to curse before he covered her clit with his mouth and sucked hard, driving his thick fingers into her core.

It was as if the most incredible aurora borealis took control of the room, starting at her core and flashing outward with brightly coloured ripples. Amber swore she heard the undulating lights sing.

Once she could breathe again, she peeled her eyes open to stare down at the big bear settled between her naked thighs. Maybe she should feel regret, or fear, or something big and scary at the huge move she'd made.

Looking into Cooper's heated gaze and the cocky grin twisting his lips, all she felt was anticipation.

A week of this? A lifetime of this, and more?

Bring it.

It was time to return the favour. Amber squirmed, planning to inch her way under him.

Or that was the idea. Instead, she found herself pinned to the bed by his weight as he stretched over her.

"You taste good." Cooper growled the words a second before he took her lips again.

She wanted to help strip away his remaining clothes.

Wanted to guide him to her and ease his pain, but his patience had vanished.

Amber found herself in his arms, held tight to his body. Her knees rested on either side of his hips, and her very wet sex lay over his thick length like a protective blanket.

"Where did your clothes go?" Amber demanded. "*When* did your clothes go?"

"Do you really care?"

Good question. Answer? Not. One. Bit.

His fingers flexed on her hips, and she rose, then fell, as he deliberately dragged her sensitive folds over his cock.

Another tingle started. Or maybe it was the lingering aftershocks of her first orgasm, but with Cooper stroking her so perfectly, round two wasn't far off.

A second later he rocked harder than before, and the head of his cock slipped between her folds. Amber sucked in a gasp.

Cooper moaned long and loud as he dropped her onto his shaft. Slowly, in control, but she felt every inch of the growing connection between them.

When she finally rested fully on his thighs, Amber offered a soft moan of her own. "Feels so good."

"Mm-hm."

Amber did an experimental squeeze of her inner muscles and couldn't stop from snickering when he cursed and started panting.

"Like that?" She did it again.

Cooper tucked his fingers under her chin and lifted. "Trouble."

"*Your* trouble. Now...are we going to sit here all day, or what?"

She should have held the teasing comment and saved

her breath to deal with the avalanche of ecstasy about to arrive.

Cooper took control. Lifting her carefully, dropping her down. Bringing their torsos close enough that his firm abdomen muscles were right there, begging for her hands. She swept her fingers over the strong ridges and muscles before leaning in all the way and making contact. His chest and her breasts meshed together, her already sensitive nipples taking the brunt of the attack.

His cock made happy little nerve endings inside her dance with delight. Each pulse seemed more deliberate, deeper, and more intense. Slowly speeding up until Amber hovered on the final edge.

She gripped his shoulder with one hand, nails digging in, and slipped the other between their bodies. Teasing the line where his cock disappeared into her, getting her fingers wet. She brought them just slightly higher and made contact with her clit.

Her knuckles grazed his abs, and his grip tightened again. Hard enough she felt each finger dig into her butt cheeks. "What do you need?" he growled. "I want to feel you come around me."

"Nearly. Nearly. More..." Amber opened her eyes and looked down. His strong body and hers were intimately twined together. A bit of light shone off the sweat on his naked torso.

His forearms rippled as he slipped one hand down and laid his fingers over hers to copy her motions and add pressure.

Those damn forearms.

Okay, playing with her clit and the fullness of his cock were also part of it, but she was totally awarding the assist for this orgasm to his forearms.

Amber decided that before she stopped thinking enough to be amused by the idea.

Cooper pumped into her one last time and held her against him, cock buried deep. Her orgasm pulsed around him, and he threw his head back and roared.

Aftershocks arrived, one rocking pulse after another, and every time her body tightened and discovered the rock-solid length still there to squeeze, she grew a little more breathless.

"Cooper? You. Didn't. Come?" One word at a time was all she was capable of.

His gaze met hers and he smiled. A sweet, caring smile as he brushed her hair back from her face and slowly angled his hips. The motion moved his heavy cock inside her, and another aftershock hit.

They both groaned.

He leaned his forehead on hers. "I came. And will again. And again, and a few more times after that. But I don't have to be inside you for all of them."

Amber blinked. The Very Blunt Talk with her friends had included this data. Sex came in a multitude of flavours, and she was going to try the entire fifty-one options before this week was over if she had any say in it.

"Whatever it takes to make you happy," she whispered. "Truly. I'm here for you, Cooper. Whatever you need."

He tilted her chin so he could examine her face carefully. Such a strange contrast of patience and pleasure, considering she was still anchored on his erection.

"I..." His eyes widened and he swore softly. "Oh, damn."

Amber paused. Okay, the whole holding a conversation while sitting on an erect cock was a new experience, but so be it. "What?"

"Birth control?" He looked moderately horrified and worried, and she hurried to reassure him.

"Covered. Well, not literally, obviously, but I'm on birth control." She poked him in the chest. "Come on. I know shifters don't carry STDs, so we didn't need a condom for that, but birth control still needs to be dealt with. You really think I'd let you near me without making you suit up otherwise?"

He relaxed for a second before something flashed in his eyes that was a whole lot hotter and wilder. His hand swept up her back and he tangled his fist in her hair, tugging to lift her face to his. "Why are you on birth control?"

Amber stilled. Cooper had asked sort of politely, but that wasn't his voice. His bear, or the wild side of him in human form, clearly wasn't pleased.

She thought back to her friends' warnings about how mating fever made guys uber-possessive. But there was a part inside her that wasn't interested in placating a hypersensitive shifter regarding *this*, not even if he were in the midst of a hormonally demanding situation.

She caught Cooper by the ears and tugged, ignoring that they were still intimately connected, and gave it to him with both barrels. "Condoms are only part of safe sex. I'm on birth control so I can have sex when I *want* to have sex. And I want to have sex with you, or I did until a few seconds ago. So, you can get growly, or you can get moving. Your choice, bucko."

It was like watching a wave roll over a shore and wipe away a mess of footprints. The tightness in his expression faded, his brow smoothed, and instead of anger, amusement rose.

"Feisty human," he muttered.

"You have no idea."

He lifted a brow. "I look forward to learning. Now, get ready for me to get moving. I plan for us to enjoy mating fever, and I've got energy to burn."

Cooper tipped them to the mattress, rearing over her.

Amber caught hold of his shoulders and held on for the ride of her life.

9

*I*t had been a good ten years that Cooper had been taking measures to avoid the fever. There'd been weeks he'd sat in his shifted form, tormented by the fever and clouds of black flies. Or freezing his butt off during snowstorms, absolutely alone except for the little creatures shivering in the woods and watching him with trepidation.

Getting free rein to do everything he wanted with Amber?

Heavenly.

He worked her over for a couple of hours that first run, most of it without a lot of talking.

Oh, there was communication going on. A lot of shouting and screaming and groaning and gasping. He particularly liked the gasping when it involved his name with "oh yes, yes, *yeeessssss*" added on.

Amber was not a particularly quiet woman, and Cooper couldn't be happier.

The vigorous sex wasn't only the thing he enjoyed,

though. The fact she'd come to him—that was important and made him feel special.

"How did you know where I was?" Cooper asked when they were temporarily paused.

"Your calendar is linked to mine," she reminded him. "It makes it easy to stalk you."

He nuzzled under her chin, curling his arms around her and pulling her closer. They were still naked, because he hadn't had nearly enough skin-on-skin time yet. He wasn't going to for a long time, and definitely not during the next week.

"I had all these plans," he confessed. "I'm glad you're here. I'm *so* glad you're here because I really wanted you to be. But I didn't think it was going to work for another few years at the earliest."

Amber slid his hand from one portion of her anatomy to another instead of trying to remove it completely. "You obviously have a list of, and you need to picture this with capital letters, Things To Deal With Before Hooking Up With Amber. You want to talk about them?"

In spite of the cuteness of her mentioning his capitalization habit, annoyance flashed. "This isn't a hookup."

Amber stilled.

Damn.

"This isn't a hookup," he repeated, this time without growling. "It's you and me working toward forever."

The tension eased out of her. She nodded decisively. "Poor wording on my part. I'm sorry. But I also know there's no guarantee. Both Lara and Kaylee told me all about their situations with James and Alex, and while I'm—"

She paused. Eyed him.

Damn again. Cooper sighed with exasperation. He lay

back on the bed and stared at the ceiling as he scolded his inner bear. *Do you mind? Growling is not a part of this current conversation. And I thought you were leaving me alone for the week after you cut and run.*

No talking about other men.

Good grief. She just said my brothers' names.

No other men.

You need to go away and let me handle this.

His bear huffed off.

Cooper tugged Amber over himself, arranging her on her back so she connected all along his front. It left her breasts available for him to palm and pet, his lips brushing her earlobe. "Okay, where were we?"

Amber laughed softly, but she arched into his palms like a kitten wanting to be petted. "Discussing why you weren't jumping my bones every time we saw each other in the office."

"Good place to start. You work for me. That's not an ideal situation for starting a relationship."

"I work for the CEO of Borealis Gems, who, I believe on paper, is still your father."

Cooper paused. "That's a tricky bit of double-talk. You do work for me. You just said it—our calendars are linked."

"If you plan on firing me for coming on to you, you'd have a war on your hands. Between your brothers, your grandfather, and all the department heads like R&D and Alex's security teams, you *try* saying I'm gone and..." She rolled over and dug her elbows into his chest. "Stop growling at me."

"It's not me," Cooper protested. "It's my damn bear."

The cutest frown twisted her expression.

"You're talking about other guys who like you. He's jealous."

"Good grief..." Amber hesitated. "He's listening to us?"

"Why shouldn't he? He's me," Cooper said before realizing that sounded a little off the wall. "It's...complicated."

"Of course it has to be complicated," she muttered softly, resting her chin in her palms. "Cooper, interoffice relationships are not a good idea when somebody's got all the power. I like working for Borealis Gems, and I like working for you, but we aren't your typical interoffice romance. Even considering you're a polar bear shifter with mating fever, I will straight up say it—I feel zero concern anyone will accuse you of pressuring me into a relationship."

"That easy?" He stroked his fingers through her hair, letting it rest over her shoulder. "Okay, as long as you promise to never leave Borealis Gems to work for anyone else without letting us counteroffer to increase your benefits and salary package."

Amber laughed softly. "Lara already tried to steal me away and I told her no. You're safe."

He'd been joking. "Seriously? Lara tried to poach you for Midnight Inc.?"

"Oops." She slapped a hand over her mouth, then winked. "Okay, let's move on to the next concern you had."

"You're trouble," Cooper said, with something near delight dancing in his belly. "And you're young."

Her eye roll was big enough to be a statement all in itself, but she followed it up with an enormous sigh of exasperation. "I can't believe you're going to try that one."

"I'm thirty-six," he pointed out.

"Congratulations."

"*Amber.*"

"*Cooper,*" she repeated back with the same tone. "I'm

twenty-five, which is younger than you, yes. But it's old enough to know my own mind. Besides, women mature faster than men, and humans *definitely* get smarter far sooner than bear shifters."

"*Hey.*" Both Cooper and his inner bear smarted at that one.

She patted his cheek saucily. "Just means you need to eat your veggies so you can keep up with me." Her expression grew solemn, sadness rising rapidly. "I can't do anything about the fact that I'm human. As far as I know, and I've done a ton of research, all those tales about finding a way to turn into a shifter are just that. Fairy tales."

"Definitely not a problem," Cooper assured her. "I have no objections to you being human, and my bear doesn't mind one bit either."

Her eyes widened for a moment, then she nodded firmly. "It means I can't share activities with you the way Kaylee and James do, or Lara and Alex. If we want to go out into the wilderness—"

"Then we find a way to go that works for us." Cooper sat up, bringing her beside him so he could look her in the eye more easily. He folded his hand around hers. "I'm not my brothers, and you're not your friends, and what we will have will be unique to us. But I already know of a very successful polar bear and human combination. They're people I look up to very much."

Amber's gaze remained fixed on his. "Your grandparents."

"Yes. And considering how long they've been together, I'm pretty sure your being human isn't going to be a problem."

He really wanted to keep talking, but it'd been nearly fifteen minutes since he'd made her squirm, and with the mating fever burning through him, that was a good fourteen minutes too long.

Besides, it seemed she'd erased most of the bullet points on his Items To Be Dealt With list in one fell swoop.

Not even twenty-four hours later, Amber took control of their food and drink situation. She'd slipped out of the shower ahead of him, and somehow by the time he reentered the main room, she was hauling a massive pile of boxes through the door.

"What's this?" He hurried to help her bring in her haul, humming in approval as the rich scent of ribs from his favourite barbecue house drifted on the air. "Oh my God, you got takeout."

"I don't know what you were thinking when you packed those coolers, but you didn't bring in enough calories for a mouse, let alone the two of us." She gestured to the porch with an imperative wave. "Go get the rest of them."

Cooper chuckled. "Yes, ma'am."

"Don't you give me sass," she warned, "or you'll be doing a whole lot more *yes, ma'am*-ing."

"Promises, promises." He snapped at the bun she threw at his head, snagging it between his teeth then growling lustily as he shook it.

Amber regally ignored him.

He moved to haul in the rest of the supplies, pausing only when she poked him with her fist. The one holding an oversized robe she'd grabbed from somewhere.

"Put this on. I like how naked looks on you, but we don't want to make anyone wandering past the cabin jealous. You're all mine."

He liked how possessive that comment sounded.

After they'd filled their bellies, he reconsidered the idea

of keeping her naked all the time and ordered her to pull on some clothes. "We both need to get outside for a while."

The sunshine pouring in the windows of the cabin was calling, and the few moments of stepping into the crisp cool December day while he was grabbing the boxes had been enough to briefly break through the mating fever.

Cooper liked being outside. Even with his desk job, he usually spent a couple of hours daily wandering in his fur, and while Amber had been a fine distraction, they both could use some fresh air.

Stretch your legs? he offered his inner bear.

Cautious interest bounced back. *This wouldn't be me breaking my promise?*

Definitely not. We're shifting to be with Amber, not to avoid her.

His bear shrugged. *You're the one with the rules.*

Cooper glanced at Amber. She had her back to him, standing in front of the mirror beside the door as she adjusted the toque on her head. She was already dressed in her boots and coat, with warm mittens sticking out of her pocket.

Perfect timing. He tossed aside his robe and shifted, stretching lazily to work out the kinks.

Amber rotated. Then she flailed backward and screamed loud enough the windows rattled.

------

10

*C*ooper sat back on his heels in utter shock.

It took a second, but Amber found her balance, back pressed to the door, hand over her chest as if she were trying to stop her heart from escaping. "Dammit, Cooper. Next time, warn a girl."

He tilted his head to the side and debated shifting back. She was still trembling. Her heart pounded loud enough he could hear it across the distance separating them, and the sharp scent of fear sliced through the air like an emergency beacon.

Inside, his bear let out a massive sigh.

Amber took a deep breath then lifted her gaze skyward. "Freaking shifters." She opened the door and gestured him out. "Come on, Cooper. Let's get that fresh air."

He moved slowly so as not to startle her again, and once they were outside, things seemed to improve immensely. Cooper stomped through the snow to create a path, and Amber followed behind. Close enough the mating fever didn't make him twitch from lack of contact but far enough that she wasn't tripping over his heels.

But he didn't follow through on his original idea, which was to make a game for them to play outside. Instead they took a simple walk together. It still felt good, but something small and tight irritated him inside—and then the mating fever flared, and he was no longer thinking about anything except the woman he wanted.

Cooper shifted on the spot.

Amber gasped in surprise, then gasped again as he reached down to catch hold of her pants in his big fists. "Cooper?"

"Is that a yes?"

She nodded immediately, thank God, because his next move was to rip her clothing apart just enough to be able to pick her up and take her on the spot, her arms and legs wrapped around him.

The winter air snapped against his naked skin, but the heat of her sex countered it perfectly, and before too long she was screaming his name, oblivious to where they were.

The next four days passed quickly, yet Cooper never felt as if they were rushed. They took long showers, followed by leisurely times where he'd dry her off with great attention to detail until her skin was glowing. Amber was a drug that called him back again and again.

It was eight days after the fever begun when Cooper knew they had reached the end. They'd curled up together on the porch swing for a final cuddle before checking out of the cabin, a heavy blanket wrapped around Amber as she leaned against his side. Her head rested on his chest as they looked over the snowy clearing they'd walked in every day.

"Cooper?"

He nuzzled his chin against the top of her hair as an answer.

She adjusted position until she could look up at him.

"What's happening with the mating fever? I mean, you're coming off the actual fever part, but has anything changed?"

He'd been dreading her asking, because something was definitely wrong. Or more specifically, nothing seemed to be right. "I have loved every minute I've spent with you, and this isn't the end, but I don't feel any different than when I started."

She responded decisively. "We knew there were no guarantees. Maybe I'm not meant to be your mate."

A sudden flash of anger hit. "Screw that. I don't give a damn what the mating fever says, you're the one I want to be with. Period."

"Cooper. You can't organize a mating like that."

He straightened, dragging her fully into his lap so he could cup her chin and stare her straight in the eye. "Watch me."

Amber shook her head. "I know how important it is to have a mate. Lara and Kaylee have told me exactly what it means, and there's no way I want you to miss out on that."

"I'm not going to miss out on anything because you *are* my mate. We obviously missed a few details along the way." He bumped his nose into hers. "Let me go talk with my bear. Maybe he has some ideas."

When Cooper nudged his inner animal, he got back an instant response.

She's got no room for me.

The statement made no sense, but it was said with such clarity Cooper figured it wasn't some off-the-cuff comment.

You got any more details to share? I want her as my mate. She says she wants the same thing, so neither of us are holding up the mating bond from kicking into place. Which means it's you...

She likes you, his bear agreed. He spoke slowly as if

reluctant to explain, but it was a necessary evil. *Likes me in safe settings, but bear is wild. She needs to love me that way too.*

Dawning comprehension arrived. There had been too many times over the years for him to not notice exactly how Amber reacted when she was around his shifted form. *You can't make someone not be afraid of you,* Cooper pointed out. *You are a big dangerous beast.*

His bear sniffed delicately. *I know that, and that's the side issue. The big issue is she has no room for me. Not yet.*

You don't make any sense, you know. After spending all that energy teasing me to get together with her, and all the possessive growling this week every time another man was mentioned, it makes no sense that you're not claiming her this instant.

I'm a bear. I don't have to be logical.

Cooper wanted to shake the beast, but Amber was looking at him with tears in her eyes, and he didn't want to prolong her agony. All he knew for sure was that he wanted to wipe away her sadness and find a solution.

But being honest was necessary. "My bear is the holdout."

Surprise danced across her face. "Oh. He doesn't like me?"

Cooper hesitated. Honesty sucked. "He's got a couple concerns. One is that you seem to be just a wee bit afraid of him."

Amber cursed softly. "I don't think he's going to hurt me, but most rational people are scared of creatures that outweigh them by over a thousand pounds. I don't think the fact that I may be a teeny bit cautious around a massive creature with fangs and claws is unreasonable."

"I totally agree," Cooper said. "We'll work it out."

She paused. "What's the other concern?"

"It's complicated. I need more details."

Amber wrapped her hands around his shoulders and leaned in close. "Then get details. I'm not going anywhere."

He kissed her first because he had to. He *needed* to, and for a few minutes their worries vanished as they connected perfectly. As he took her lips and gave her 100 percent acknowledgement that she was perfect for him.

That she was who he chose.

Her lips were swollen and she was smiling faintly when he pulled back. "We'll find a way. This is just a glitch in the system. A bug. A temporary hiccup," he assured her.

"Of epic proportions," she said, but she blinked, her gaze clearing to meet his straight on. "I trust you."

The thrill that went through him was bigger than their problem. "That means everything to me."

Amber wiped at her eyes before a steely determination firmed her expression. "Okay, bucko. We need to make a list. You talk to that stubborn bear of yours and find out the details, and then we'll make this happen."

11

*A*mber stared around Cooper's living room at the supplies gathered in heaps. "I don't know how I'm going to repay you for getting all of this together so quickly," she said to Lara.

Her friend waved it off. "You know we'd do anything to help, so stop with the grateful bullshit, and let's figure out the rest of the details."

In the far corner of the room, Cooper and his brothers were poring over a set of maps, a lively discussion between them.

Kaylee slipped her arm around Amber and squeezed. "What Lara said. The sooner Cooper's bear is satisfied, the sooner you officially become family. And while I like being best friends, I'm going to be very happy to have you as a sister-in-law."

"Ditto." Lara lifted her gaze to the person who stood in the doorway, knocking on the frame. "Dixon. Did you find more information?"

The lanky wolf shifter sauntered into the room. He gave his Alpha a polite acknowledgement before offering Amber a wink. "My contact says it was definitely Mason he saw. I've got the coordinates."

Thank goodness. Amber pointed him toward the corner where the guys were. "Show them. They're figuring out the travel logistics."

She took a deep breath and worked to calm herself.

After a week of sexual bliss, it had been rough to have her dreams dashed so suddenly. But they weren't without hope—when Cooper's bear had finally spilled the beans in a way that they could all understand, it had turned out his cryptic *she's got no room for me* complaint centered around the fact Amber was still looking for her missing brother.

A stab slid through her heart. As wonderful as the possibilities before her were, sadness lingered. For years she'd alternated between sorrow and fear at having lost track of her brother. At not knowing what had happened to her foster parents.

Yet every time she doubted she'd ever discover what had happened to them, hope had crept in. Maybe she was silly to feel so certain that they were all okay, especially after so long, but the sensation remained. That sense deep down that she knew they were out there, somewhere, and that everything was fine.

She needed to sell shares in Optimists "R" Us.

"I need to find Mason. That part has always been true, but now so much more is tangled up in achieving that goal," Amber said to Kaylee before confessing, "I'm scared. Just a little."

Kaylee offered an encouraging hug. "I get it. Really, I do. Because this is something that's important to you, and Cooper, and to your future. It's important because of your past. But you will make it happen. None of us is going to stop until you get your happily ever after."

Curses burst out from the corner where the guys were, and Amber and her friends turned to face them, concern rising.

"What?" Amber demanded.

Cooper's expression was grim. "According to this, we're looking at a shifter settlement north of Ghost Lake."

"That's good." Amber paused because no one else seemed excited by the news. "That's bad?"

"I can't fly you there," James told her bluntly. "The hills and the wind off the lake mix in a way that's not great for aircraft. No one goes in or out of there by flying."

"It would take a miracle to get a plane in," Alex agreed. "The only way to get there is to run."

"Or be pulled by runners," James suggested.

Confusion. Amber turned to Kaylee. "What are they talking about?"

Her friend looked concerned as well. "There are a lot of shifter villages that aren't accessible by air. Which is a bit of a problem for you unless you're okay with not arriving until next spring."

Lara tugged on Kaylee's sleeve to get her attention. "What about if she used a dogsled?"

Kaylee nodded thoughtfully. "That could work. If Amber knew how to drive one. Oh, and if she could find a spare sled and some dogs."

A sudden rush of having this under control struck. "Dogsled would be fine, and I know exactly where to find some sleds. Borealis Gems is storing extras for one of the teams we sponsored for the Iditarod."

"And sled dogs?"

In the corner of the room, Dixon perked up, his hand shooting into the air. "Oh, oh. Pick me, pick me!"

Alex looked confused for a second before obviously

communicating silently with Lara to figure out what Dixon was talking about.

Then Cooper's brother rolled his eyes and muttered, "Damn wolf hearing," before folding his arms across his chest and turning toward the overeager wolf. "Dixon Mallory, we've talked about this. The Orion pack has got to stop acting like animals. Pulling dogsleds is beneath the dignity of a shifter."

"Screw dignity, it would be a hell of a good time," Dixon said with a grin.

"Lara," Alex said, looking to her for backup.

His mate shrugged. "No help here, sweetie. I agree. I'm totally willing to dogsled it for Amber, not only because I think she's awesome, but it *would* be a hell of a good time."

Even as Alex fought to keep a stern expression, Dixon rolled with the idea and slapped a hand on Cooper's shoulder. "I can get a team of volunteers together for you, stat, no problem, man."

He backed off instantly, hands raised in a protective fashion as Cooper bared his teeth.

Quickly, though, the snarl turned into a smile, and Cooper offered Dixon his hand. "We would appreciate it very much. Find enough for two sleds, and Amber and I will make it worth your while."

"Like I said, the adventure's the reason to do it." Dixon pulled out his phone, tapping rapidly at the screen. "Let me talk to my guys."

Amber joined Cooper on the other side of the room.

The entire conversation had taken place in a whirlwind but left one point of confusion. "What do you mean two sleds? Are you coming with me?"

Cooper went absolutely still. "Of course I'm going with

you. You didn't really think I was going to leave you to track down your brother by yourself?"

"I didn't think your bear wanted to be with me," she admitted.

Instantly his eyes changed as the wild side of him came to the forefront. The bear nature was there no matter what form he took, but now even more blatantly—that was not human intelligence staring back. "You're still mine. You're not going anywhere without me."

Amber fought to keep from grinning. Cooper's complaints about how illogical his bear could be shone clearly at that moment.

And then she figured, screw it. She was amused, and thankful, and both sides of him needed to know that. She wrapped her arms around him and squeezed tight. Hugging the bear as much as the man. "I'm glad I'm yours, and we will figure this out so that we can *all* be happy together."

Was it irrational to talk to one part of Cooper while holding on to another? Getting involved with the shifter world meant suspending a lot of expectations.

It took until the next day to track down the sleds, move all of the supplies, and meet with the group of wolf shifters Dixon had assembled.

Alex still looked a little disgruntled but waved it off when Amber asked why he was pouting. "I need to get over myself. Last night the damn wolf pack set up a lottery to decide who won the privilege of being your escorts."

Amber wrapped him up in a big tight hug. "I promise not to call them good doggies or anything like that."

She only stayed in his arms for an instant before Cooper silently caught her by the wrist and pulled her free, possessively wrapping her in his embrace and glaring at his brother.

It was Lara who answered with a snicker. "Oh, you go right ahead and call them anything you want. You could get away with murder right now. Someone suggested we should erect an altar to you in the pack house. Amber—goddess of fun winter activities."

The other surprise as they headed outside to the loaded sleds—Kaylee and James were there as well. They stood in the snow in robes, obviously waiting to shift and join the group.

"What're you doing?" Amber asked. "I thought you were taking care of my job while I go gallivanting."

A familiar voice sounded from behind them. "I used to act as the CEO's secretary, back in the day. I'm perfectly capable of keeping the difficult man in charge under control while you track down your family."

Amber turned to discover Cooper's grandparents standing together, Giles's arm wrapped around Laureen. "Mrs. Borealis?"

"Isn't that a little formal, my dear? When Kaylee told me what was going on, Giles and I offered to step in for the duration." She slipped forward, lifting Amber's hood around her face and tucking her hair in. A very caring and grandmotherly gesture that nearly took Amber's feet out from under her. "You need your friends with you as you start this journey. Don't worry about us. We'll take care of things."

Grandfather Giles stepped forward as well, his eyes twinkling like always. "No use arguing when she gets an idea in her head. Heaven knows I don't try." He leaned forward and gave Amber a kiss on the cheek, then glared at Cooper, who had marched forward instinctively. "Don't you growl at your grandfather."

Cooper grinned, all teeth and rumbling noises. "Thank you for your help."

Amber turned to Kaylee. Her friend smiled and stepped forward to embrace her. "What Grandma said. You need your friends with you." She lowered her voice. "And an adventure running across the tundra? Dixon was right. It's going to be a hell of a good time."

They both laughed, the sound welling up around the group.

As if summoned by speaking his name, Dixon appeared beside them with a happy sigh. "This is so awesome. Although, you know, the one thing we're missing is theme music. Something to get the blood pumping before a good hard run."

Others of the pack gathered closer, drawn like flies to honey by Dixon's enthusiasm.

"Although, sometimes that backfires. Like when you get an earworm, and you only know two lines of the entire song and that's all you think of for hours on end." Dixon's grin hovered on maniacal. "Once, I got that song from *Shrek* in my head. You know, the one with *rock star* and..."

Panic filled the wolves' eyes as Dixon started humming the catchy tune.

"He's terrible," Amber whispered admiringly to Cooper, wondering how the young man had survived this long.

Suddenly everywhere people were getting naked, and Amber was trying to find a safe place to look without looking. The wolves slipped into their shifter-friendly harnesses that Lara explained would allow them to detach themselves when they wanted to get free. Final packages were being strapped to the sleds.

James and Kaylee shifted, the bobcat pouncing on her

mate in what look like an entirely reckless move considering he was so much larger than her.

But as always, James was kind and gentle with his mate. He dropped willingly to his back, paws in the air as if he were a dead bug so Kaylee could give his face a tongue bath.

It was so much to take in. All these people were gathered to help her. Her and Cooper. There was life and laughter, and under it that lingering sense of sadness.

Yet as always—hope.

Amber twisted toward the gentle giant who was doing the final checks on his sled. As if sensing her gaze, Cooper left his task to return to her side and catch her against him in a giant bear hug.

He brushed their noses together. "Are you ready?"

With a death grip around his neck, she kissed him. Fiercely, possessively. With every bit of the emotion that had been filling her chest for the past hours and days and months and years, if she was being honest.

Sweet words hovered on her tongue, but she kept them back because a howling and whistling wolf pack was not the best audience for her first declaration of love for Cooper.

But it was true. She loved him.

The words would keep, but the feeling was there, warming her from the inside out. She pulled back and was happy to note that Cooper wore a glassy-eyed expression and looked as befuddled as she felt.

"With you? I'm ready for anything."

12

*H*e'd worried at first. Because of course he did.

Still, he should've known that Amber hadn't been blowing smoke when she said she could handle the dogsled, and he didn't think it was because the dogs were actually shifters.

They'd headed out of town as quickly as possible, finding the open route to the north and west. Amber led the way, with Lara as her lead on the line of wolves hauling the sled forward. This was still familiar territory for the Orion pack, and Cooper wasn't at all concerned that they would get off the trail. Not with his sister-in-law guiding them.

He opened the line between his and Amber's headsets. "You're handling the sled just fine."

"I took lessons back in the spring. Didn't realize it was going to come in handy so soon, but yeah. I know what I'm doing." Ahead of him, she glanced over her shoulder for a moment. The line crackled and then she continued. "You're not so bad yourself. You do this often?"

"Grandmother insisted we all learn survival skills. Because as she put it, 'even you seemingly indestructible polar bears might occasionally need other forms of transportation.'"

"She's the one who gave me the lessons as a present. It's obviously something she's passionate about." Amber's voice held a smile. "I like your grandma."

"She's your grandmother now too," he insisted. Then he changed the topic before she could protest. "Are you warm enough?"

"If I'm not, I can just run more and ride less."

Cooper admired the view as the landscape unfolded. The snow was hard-packed and windblown, and they had reached the point where they could travel side by side.

The wolves who weren't attached to the ropes ran out and back willy-nilly, tongues hanging from their mouths as they grinned with sheer delight. James and Alex ran as well, their lumbering bear forms a sharp contrast with the sleek wolves and the dainty bobcat also keeping pace.

Cooper glanced over at Amber, but she was focused on her task. She didn't seem the least bit afraid or fazed by the fact she was surrounded by a whole squadron of shifters in their wild forms.

She's doing well, he pointed out to his inner bear.

Of course she is. You need to stop assuming that I think she's wrong for us. She's just not ready for us, that's all.

She's awfully willing to jump through hoops for being not ready, Cooper said with a touch of annoyance.

While he understood how important it was to find Amber's brother, this whole delay on completing the mating bond had left a sizzle of frustration running just under his skin. As if the lack of finishing up was somehow making the situation worse.

His bear vanished, and Cooper settled back into concentrating on the task at hand.

They stopped a few times to let everyone rest and switch out the wolves who needed a break.

And to eat. Everyone needed to eat.

The weather was cooperating, the sky overhead blue with wisps of clouds that stretched like ribbons across the wide expanse. Crisp cold made each breath fresh and sharp. It was a glorious day for an outing, and with everyone along, it was more like a party than a serious venture.

Amber pulled food supplies from her sled and passed them out, wandering calmly into the middle of the pack, amidst the wolves. Lara and Kaylee had shifted back, dressed quickly against the cold, and helped her. James and Alex shifted as well and came to join Cooper as he prepared a lunch for everyone not still in their fur.

None of the breaks were for very long, and it still took most of the day to cover the distance to the small village.

They pulled into the clearing in the middle of the square, and a greeting committee met them.

An older woman stepped forward, eyeing the group with curiosity. "Welcome. I'm Chief Starling. Are you looking for a place to stay?"

Amber stepped forward. "Possibly. But also, I'm trying to track down my brother, Mason Myawayan. We heard he might've been here."

The woman frowned. "I think I remember that name, but it was a while back."

Cooper wrapped an arm around Amber and squeezed in encouragement. "If he was here, we might be able to figure out where he went next. If you have any way of checking your records, we would appreciate it."

A whispered conversation was taking place amongst a group of children who had gathered. They watched with fascination as each wolf pack member slipped out of their own harness then trotted off after the locals guiding them to places to spend the night.

But now a small girl came forward, slipping her hand into the elder's before looking up for permission to speak.

The woman offered a smile before turning to Amber. "My granddaughter." She looked at the little girl. "Do you remember something, Jessie?"

The girl nodded instantly. "I can show you. I think it was him."

Jessie took Amber's hand in hers then, to Cooper's shock, she boldly grabbed his hand as well, tugging them both toward what had to be a common gathering house.

"It was a long time ago, but I remember him because he had the same smiling eyes you have. Not just a smile on his lips, but here." She tapped the side of her head. "As if his happiness was shining out on all of us."

Jessie paused outside the door of a large community center before guiding them into a playroom.

Cooper followed as Jessie headed to a bookshelf and pulled down an artist's notebook. Inside there were more than a dozen sketches of the children of the community. Some showed them playing, others depicted them working with their families.

All of them were signed by Mason, with the date from approximately a year earlier.

Amber ran a finger over the page. "He was here. And yes, he has smiling eyes," she told Jessie before opening her arms to offer a hug. "Thank you for showing me these. It makes it feel as if I'm closer to him than I was before."

The little girl slipped into Amber's embrace and squeezed.

Cooper watched as Amber closed her eyes and seemed to soak in strength from the sweet exchange.

It was nearly an hour later by the time all the wolves had found showers and clothing, and everyone gathered together to discuss what came next.

"My children checked the records to see if there was anything recorded about where Mason planned to go next. As far as we can tell, he took the northeastern trade route toward the Arctic coast. He promised to drop off packages with some of our family along the way." Chief Starling leaned her elbows on the table. "I can offer you the same help we gave him. Some skidoos, and directions to supply stops."

Before Amber could say anything, because she was obviously eager to accept, Cooper spoke up. "How long a journey is it?"

The old woman considered. "A week? Maybe a few days more or a few days less depending on the weather."

Cooper turned to Amber, ignoring the murmur in the background as the information trickled down to the wolves. "If you want to do this, I'll go with you, but I don't think we can expect everyone else to come along."

She tangled her fingers in his where they lay in his lap. "I know, and it's wonderful to have them here, but as long as you come with me, we'll be okay."

He lifted their joined hands and kissed her knuckles. "Of course I'm coming with you. That was never in question."

"I knew that too." She squeezed his fingers then turned back to the table and the head of the clan. "Your offer is very generous, and we appreciate it very much."

Chief Starling nodded then clapped her hands to get the attention of the assembled group. "Since you will be staying the night, I guess we should have a party. If I can get some volunteers to help get ready?"

She was swarmed by wolves then laughed as she pointed them in a dozen different directions.

Cooper found himself alone with his brothers as Kaylee and Lara stole Amber away.

Alex looked him over then nodded. "It's pretty much what I expected you to do at some point. Ride off into the wilderness, looking for answers."

"I didn't think you'd be doing it with a human," James said, "but Amber's perfect for you. I hope this works out."

Cooper shook his hand and patted him on the back the way brothers do—i.e. nearly hard enough to knock James's lungs out. "Of course it's going to work out. Now go make sure Alex's wolves aren't getting into mischief."

"Why are they *my* wolves when they're being bad? How come they're not Lara's wolves?" Alex complained.

Cooper just raised a brow.

As soon as James trotted off and they were alone, though, Alex's expression turned serious. "Are you feeling okay?"

Strange question. "Pretty much. I'm probably in better shape than you considering I got to ride a sled today instead of running my ass off."

Alex shook his head. "That's not what I'm asking. How's your bear? I did some research about the mating bond after I was stupid and nearly messed things up with Lara. I ended up following a rabbit trail that led me to some information that's kind of worrisome. I didn't mention it before because I hoped we'd find Mason right away and things would be done, but it looks as if you've still got a long journey ahead of you."

Cooper considered. That electric itch was still there under his skin. That was the only thing that seemed out of the norm. "My bear side has his reasons for holding off on mating. I can't fault him for that, and we're dealing with it as quickly as possible."

His brother lowered his voice. "Just be careful. From what I read, when it's the shifter holding back and it goes on for too long, one of two things can happen. Either he'll end up taking total control, or you'll have to. Permanently."

Dear God. "Do you mean to say—?"

"If you don't finish the mating bond in time, you could get stuck as a bear. Or you could end up as a human, never able to shift again. And the longer you wait, the less choice you'll have in which it will be."

13

The evening passed in a blur, and Amber found herself smiling an extraordinary amount.

There was food and drink and dancing. A few members of the Orion wolf pack seemed intent on doing all three at the same time, which meant it was dangerous out on the dance floor.

Her friends were there, and the laughter and warmth of the time was made better because Kaylee and Lara were happy as well. They each took turns dancing with their mates, and the adoring expressions on James's and Alex's faces as they stared at their partners made every bit of hopefulness in Amber's heart flare.

When it was her turn to be in Cooper's arms, it was one step shy of perfect.

She sighed happily and rested her cheek against his chest as he guided her around the floor.

"For a small person, you can make an awful lot of noise," Cooper teased.

She glanced up and grinned. "I thought that was something you liked about me. How noisy I am."

Hunger flashed in his eyes, and the next thing she knew, they were leaving the gathering hall. She was draped over his shoulder, her face hot as could be, but in spite of the catcalls chasing after them, she didn't care.

She cared even less when he quickly found the room they'd been given, stripped off her clothing, and proceeded to tenderly make love to her.

When they were done, both still breathing heavily, Cooper curled himself around her and held her tight. Stroking her hair and petting her as if he couldn't get enough.

"Are you really ready to head into the wilderness? Just the two of us?" he asked quietly.

Amber rolled in his arms, looking up into the shiny depths of his deep blue eyes. "There are parts of it that scare me, but not the fact that we'll be together. And I feel it—this sense that everything we need is just around the corner. I'm not going to give up on us, Cooper."

"I'm not going to, either. There is nothing that can stop me from being with you forever. I don't care what it takes, or what sacrifices have to be made, we *will* be together."

She kept the smile mostly off her lips. He sounded so dramatic in that moment, a far cry from the logical and step-by-step lawyer she'd been around for so many months. "Let's try to avoid the sacrifice bit, okay? And just so we're clear, yes, I know how to drive a skidoo. Another thing I learned living with my foster parents."

Cooper leaned up on an elbow. "They sound as if they were pretty amazing."

"*Are* amazing." She nodded decisively. "As soon as we find Mason, he'll be able to tell us more. I don't think they're gone for good, I really don't."

His grin was bright and happy. "You're such an

optimist. It's a good trait. To look for the hope. To feel as if things will turn out okay."

She dragged her fingers down his chest slowly, teasing and touching because she could. "To *know* things will turn out okay." She arched a brow and looked at him questioningly. "Do you know how to drive a sled?"

He nodded.

A sneaking suspicion slipped in. "Grandmother Laureen?"

"But of course. Grandfather, too, but he usually ran along in his bear form while she used the sled. We used to do slalom races against her, and more than half the time, we'd lose—that woman is fearless."

Cooper kept talking late into the night, sharing stories about his family and his grandparents. Times with his brothers when they made mischief and all the times they'd spent learning together.

It felt as if he was trying to share everything that was important to him and the words kept spilling out.

Amber didn't want to interrupt, so she held on tight and listened and simply soaked it all in. She fell asleep with his voice in her ears, Cooper murmuring softly about love and family and choices.

A cold wind greeted them in the morning as they prepared for the next stage of the journey, beginning with saying goodbye.

Kaylee gave her a hug. "Stay safe and get in touch when you can. I hope you find Mason soon."

"Thanks. And you run fast on the way home. You don't want to get frostbite."

Lara gave Amber a tackle squeeze before ruffling her hair then pulling her toque back on. "We'll be fine. We have big polar bears to cuddle with if it gets too cold."

"My cute furry baby is like the world's biggest hot water bottle." Kaylee glanced at Amber. "Remember that. If the weather gets too cold, tell Cooper to shift and use him as your own personal heating device."

"It's easier than slicing open a tauntaun," Lara agreed.

"And they smell much better," Amber and Kaylee said at the same time before bursting into laughter.

Cooper was saying goodbye to his brothers where they waited beside the wolf pack. He stood patiently while Dixon got in an overzealous hug, then Cooper shook Alex's hand in a strangely solemn manner.

With a final thanks to the village and the chief, Amber and Cooper were off, skidoos gliding over the shimmering whiteness that stretched as far as the eye could see.

The sun played peekaboo behind the clouds. When it snuck out, Amber was grateful for the sun goggles protecting her from the brilliant glare reflecting off the surfaces all around her. It was like being inside a shiny bowl and having slivers of light shooting at her from every direction.

Shortly after noon they found the first refueling station, filling their machines then taking a break a little further down the trail. A wide stretch of river wove back and forth, completely covered by ice. On the inner corner, though, a number of holes had been opened in the frozen surface, and it was clear someone had been ice fishing recently.

Cooper eyed the frozen river with what was definitely a wistful expression.

Amber laughed. "You're so transparent sometimes. Did you want to stop for a while?"

He jerked upright in surprise. "I don't have to. It would slow us down too much."

She shrugged. "I don't know that we're in a race against

time. Either Mason will be around when we get there, or he won't. There's nothing to say we can't travel at a pace that works for us. Which means why don't you fish? It'll save some of our food supplies for another day."

Cooper nodded slowly. "I don't think we should dawdle too much, but you're right. It would save us food." He glanced at her. "I'll have to shift."

Here they went. Ever since he'd surprised her back at the cabin, Amber had been waiting for an opportunity to make this point.

She went straight into his personal space, planted her fists on her hips and stared him in the eye. "I assumed you would shift because I don't think you're any better at catching them with your human hands than I am, and I don't remember us packing fishing gear."

He slowly shrugged out of his coat, laying it over the seat of the sled. "I don't want to make things tougher for you. That's all."

"Maybe part of the reason why your bear and I are a little uncomfortable around each other is because we've never had the chance to *get* comfortable. Have you ever thought about that?"

He went absolutely still. Opened his mouth. Closed it.

He tilted his head, and suddenly it was his bear examining her as his eyes changed slightly to reveal the wilder part of him.

She lifted a hand to his face, the roughness of his beard already beginning to appear. "I'm not scared of you." She spoke softly but clearly. "I'm cautious, and that's not the same thing as scared. Maybe if we spend more time together, that caution will go away."

Amber helped strip off Cooper's shirt, and this time it wasn't with some sexual haze but a determination to learn more about both sides of this amazing man she wanted in her life.

Although how shifters could stand in an icy wind with bare feet on the snow was beyond her.

She stepped back slightly, but kept her gaze fixed as Cooper met her eyes directly one more time. He nodded as if agreeing and then—

It was indescribable. That moment of transitioning between human and animal. His magic seemed to blur the forms so at the same time he was Cooper the man and Cooper the bear, and yet neither.

When the magic settled, a massive polar bear with blue eyes rested on his haunches only a few feet away from her, sitting very, very still.

Which was considerate, because no matter how much she wanted to prove she accepted both sides of this man, *whoa, Nellie*, he was big.

Big head, big paws. Big body now settling to the ice as he rested his chin between his front paws and looked up at her.

Waiting.

Amber marched forward, dipping low enough she could brush a hand through the thick fur on the top of his head and his neck. Slowly she worked her way around him, getting used to the feel of his fur under her fingers. Estimating the distance around his torso and deciding that if push came to shove, she could probably ride him—not that she was going to say that out loud.

When she finished her leisurely stroll around the behemoth that was Cooper, she returned to his head. "Okay. I have zero desire to arm wrestle you in this form, but I can see why the girls call their mates cute."

Cooper lifted his head, disapproval apparent in his eyes.

"Sorry, but it's true. I mean, you're also intimidating and massive and a mighty predator, *grrrr* and growl and all that. But gosh, you're also cute."

The bear pulled back his lips into a smile and razor-sharp teeth came into view.

Amber had been expecting it, so while her heart rate picked up a little, she knew it was all in fun. "Don't sneak up on me, that's all I'm saying. I might tackle hug you."

Cooper the bear rolled his eyes so hard he ended up on his back, legs waggling in the air.

Amber gathered her courage and slipped beside him, leaning into his side and laughing.

Connection growing.

14

*C*ooper was head over heels in love.

He was also standing knee-deep in the open water of the riverbank where Amber had ordered him to get fishing, but all in all, he was very pleased with how the past few minutes had gone.

Isn't she awesome? he asked his bear.

The creature rumbled a little, slightly distracted by the fish darting below the surface. Mostly not wanting to admit the truth.

Go on. Admit it. Amber is awesome, and she totally dealt with your big furry ass without freaking out. Maybe there was a way to shortcut the mating situation before any of the dire issues Alex had mentioned became true.

I like her, his bear admitted. *She's trying, but she needs to find her brother. Otherwise she's going to spend all her time wondering where her family is instead of becoming our family.*

And there again, Cooper couldn't argue with the logic. Which was annoying, considering his bear's stance on logic.

For the next fifteen minutes, he gave in to the other side and thoroughly enjoyed chasing the silvery salmon. Once he had a nice selection, he sat down and waited to see what Amber would do.

She'd had been watching him fish, and she stepped forward right away. Her approval was clear as she stooped over the pile of fish still quivering on the riverbank then nodded at him. "Very nice fish. Well done."

Okay, she is kinda cute when she's trying to suck up, his bear said.

But then the damn creature had to go and shake.

A shout of dismay rang out from Amber. By the time Cooper pulled himself back together and shifted to human, it was to discover her glaring at him. Water dripped off the end of her nose and from the ends of her sleeves.

He shrugged. "Oops?"

Amber rolled her eyes at him then shook herself, rather unsuccessfully in his estimation. "Fine. Get dressed and you can help me deal with the fish."

Which was when Cooper discovered that despite all the training his grandmother had insisted he and his brothers complete while in human form, parts of his education were lacking.

The fire did nothing but smolder. Plus, when he picked up a fish to help Amber clean it, he had no idea what to do.

Amber had watched him as closely in his human form as she'd examined his animal side, and now she pushed his hands aside and took over the fish. "I'll work on teaching you later. Now we should have something to eat quickly and then hit the trail again."

"But there's no fire," Cooper growled, annoyed with himself on so many levels.

"We don't need a fire now, and if we don't manage to get one going tonight, that's okay. You'll just have to keep me warm," Amber told him. "I'm pretty sure between you and that set of high-quality sleeping bags, I'm going to end up toasty warm."

She'd been working quickly while she spoke and now handed him a plate covered with beautifully sliced ribbons of salmon sashimi.

Cooper pretended to be shocked. "I can't eat that. It's raw."

She stared at him in horror. "You're kidding me, right?"

How he kept his expression straight, he didn't know. "Raw food? That's for bears."

Don't mind if I do. His animal side poked him eagerly.

Amber slid into his lap, one brow raised as she examined him. Then she shook her head and grinned. "You're a tease."

He let a smile come as he used his fingers to pick up one of the delicate morsels. He lifted it to her mouth. "Eat."

Her lips closed around his fingers. Her tongue stroked hot and wet against him until she pulled back and began chewing.

Cooper took the next piece for himself and commanded his body to behave until the food was gone, because then there would be no reason for them to continue to sit there in the cold. Not when she was looking at him with those eyes that said the sooner they got to where they'd set up for the night and they could get truly warmed up, the better.

Travel fell into an easy rhythm. They woke, ate, packed, and traveled. Through it all, they chatted when they could, headsets buzzing with shared stories and hopes and dreams.

It was lonely out on the tundra, the landscape changing only minutely once they passed beyond the tree line. There were sections with more rocks, or more hills, or the occasional lake with scraggy brush clinging to the shoreline. But whiteness and blue skies and small bushes covered with more whiteness were pretty much it.

The fuel caches were in good repair, but with each one they reached, Cooper scented less activity in the recent past.

They were going through their supplies at a steady rate, so whenever possible, he shifted to fish. Amber didn't seem to be at all upset by his animal presence.

They were setting up for the third night when he caught her tossing a rope over one of the scarce trees in the vicinity.

"What are you doing?" Cooper asked.

"Hanging our food, same as usual."

He knew he was staring. He'd had no idea she'd been doing that. "Why?"

"To keep it from wild animals."

"You're adorable." The words slipped out before he could stop them.

She paused. "Um... Thank you? But why?"

He caught her chin in his fingers. "The biggest, baddest predator out here is me."

She blinked. "Oh." Another pause, then she nodded.

Cooper hesitated. If she looked horrified...

A sharp sound escaped her lips. Cooper checked carefully to discover Amber was laughing.

"Oh my God, your face. I can *totally* see why Kaylee and Lara say that polar bears are cute."

"Oh, honey, no. We're the scariest of all the beasts."

"But cute... I think it's the winking." She gave him an exaggerated example, and he snickered in return.

I do not look like that when I wink, his inner bear protested, but the animal was snickering as well.

The fourth day of the journey, they hit a snag. This fuel cache had been used lately, and only a limited amount of supplies were left.

Amber eyed the skimpy stockpile. "If we fill both our sleds, somebody else is going to hit this stop and be in big trouble." She glanced at him. "What if I take the sled, and you run along in your bear form? We can hook a small toboggan behind me for anything extra we want to take, but then we'll only have to fuel one vehicle."

"Are you sure?"

"I'm the one who suggested it," Amber said dryly. "Come on. It makes the most sense, as long as your bear is up to it, which I'm pretty sure he is, because he's awesome."

Why is it that I know she's buttering me up, yet it still feels good when she makes a compliment? This is a human thing, correct?

It was damn amusing is what it was.

It was also hopeful because as long as his bear was still trying to figure things out, Cooper thought he wouldn't be making any rash decisions like trying to take over full time.

It's a human thing, he agreed. *It means she likes you. Humans also deal with this by teasing the people they want to spend time with. And occasionally poking each other. Only that one gets complicated as to who gets to poke who, when, without overstepping boundaries.*

Humans are weird.

No arguments there.

Which is how Cooper and Amber ended up abandoning one of the sleds and heading out. A skid full of extra supplies was attached behind Amber's sled, and Cooper, in his fur, bounded along at her side.

There was something exhilarating about having the snow under his feet as they raced forward. Amber drove the sled with confidence, the occasional dip or rise hidden by the sheer strength of the sun on the snow occasionally sending her jerking. But she kept her seat, and they made good time.

Darkness welled near the distant horizon.

Cooper moved toward Amber to make sure she'd spotted the change in the coming weather. She was already focusing on the sky. She waved a hand forward, gesturing to the right where the faintest shadow suggested there might be trees or a place to find shelter from the coming storm.

The wind picked up. Cooper tucked his head down and put all his energy into moving forward. Beside him, Amber fought the wind and the increasingly rough terrain.

They were still too far from the protective shelter of the ridge when the wind unexpectedly changed direction. It picked up the layer of snow that had been on top of the base, and suddenly they were surrounded by whiteout conditions.

Between one breath and the next, Cooper lost sight of Amber.

He slowed, keen ears listening for the sound of the sled engine. The steady buzz slowed as Amber dropped speed—

A grinding whine rang out. Cooper cursed because he knew the noise. The shocking sound of the engine whining at high speed followed by a muffled crumple as if a paper bag were being folded against a snowy mattress.

Amber.

He moved quickly, the tumbled skid the first thing he discovered. A few feet away, the sled lay on its side. The engine was still whining, smoke billowing from the electrical system.

He put his nose down and tracked straight to Amber.

She lay so still and motionless he was nearly scared to death. He stuck his nose beside her neck and was delighted when she shouted, rolling and scooting away from him, crab-like.

"Dammit, Cooper. I told you not to sneak up on me." She pressed her hand to her forehead and swayed.

He shifted, catching her in his arms. "Sorry about the nose. I know it's cold."

She laughed softly then moaned. "Okay. Next move?"

Cooper glanced around quickly. He spotted a gear bag that had been tossed off the skid and hauled it back to her side. By some freak luck, he'd found the sack holding their sleeping bags, and he wrapped the warm fabric around her. "Stay here. I'm going to make a basic snow cave. I'll go as fast as I can."

When she didn't protest, he stepped away and shifted again so he could use all fours and his full bear power to dig into the snow. The wind whistled past, but as soon as he broke through the upper layers and got down a foot or two, the hard snow beside him created a wind block. The temperature was still cold but lessened without the windchill.

In the distance, the sled engine hiccuped then stalled.

By the time he made the pit deep enough for the two of them and went back in his human form, Amber had dragged together a few more of their supplies.

Concern and cold hung on her. "I can't find our shelter."

"We'll be okay," he promised, reaching for the clothing she'd found for him.

She pushed his hand away. "You need to shift. If you

stay in your bear, you'll keep both of us a whole lot warmer."

"Are you sure?"

Amber nodded decisively. "I'm positive."

Shift. You're not built for this weather. I am, his bear said bluntly. *Hurry up.*

The urge to change was so strong, Cooper worried that it wasn't a good idea. Was his bear taking over?

Yet shifting made the most sense, so he led her back to the basic shelter, helped her down and arranged the blankets so that once he was in his bear form, they'd both be as protected as possible.

"No slicing me open like a tauntaun," he warned.

He wasn't sure why she laughed as hard as she did.

Laughter still on her lips, Amber caught hold of his face and kissed him fiercely before leaning back against the snowy wall and wrapping the sleeping bag tighter around herself. She watched him shift and, once he had carefully settled, she crawled up against him.

She shivered hard, her face screwed up tight. It was breaking his heart that she was so afraid but still willing to face her fears.

Why did it take you so long to shift? his bear asked. *Even I was cold out there,* he complained.

Probably not a good thing to discuss that they might have a possible issue at hand, Cooper decided. If it came down to it, he would stay in human form to be with Amber forever.

It was a terrible decision to imagine making, but ever since he'd heard Alex's warning, Cooper had been quietly considering his options.

Yet as the temperature around them slowly rose and Amber rolled in to face his chest, she reached out a hand

and brushed against him. And again. As if she was petting him as she fell asleep.

That little bit of hope in his heart grew larger. Maybe, just maybe, everything was going to work out okay, and no one would need to make any big sacrifices.

15

*A*mber woke to a low buzz in her ears and the heat of a sultry summer day.

A pale blue light filtered from above, and when she twisted her head, she discovered the groundsheet that they'd stretched over them before curling up against the storm was now firmly anchored in place by snow.

They were safe and cozy in their small snow cave, and she was no longer cuddled up against Cooper's bear, but his very human self.

Naked self.

Naked and *aroused* self—that last bit became utterly apparent in a very short period of time. He moved her over him, and she blinked in surprise at discovering his back rested on a soft surface that was warm to the touch.

"Where did you find a bed?" she asked.

"The one supply bag I tossed in the hole with us had exactly what we needed. Once we had a roof overhead, and it warmed up, I shifted and did a little organizing. You were sleeping soundly, so I guess you missed the action." He stroked his hand over her cheek and down the side of her neck. "How do you feel? Anything hurt after your little flight off the sled?"

She stretched slowly, the heat from his body sliding around her like a radiator. "A few twinges, but nothing serious. How are *you* this morning?"

His eyes flashed, wild and needy. "Hungry."

He slid his hand up her back and pressed her body closer to his, angling their mouths together for a kiss. The setting was unlike anywhere she'd ever experienced before. The blue light shining down on them was still visible even with her eyes closed, turning her surroundings into something unworldly.

Cooper kept her anchored, though, his kiss bringing her to here and now. Exactly where she wanted to be. His touch was so caring, so careful, and the love growing in her heart welled up even stronger.

The two years of admiring him had been a lead-up to now. These past days getting to spend time with him—with Cooper *and* his bear— had been the missing piece.

Cooper the man was everything she desired. He was smart and sexy and caring. Cooper the bear was equally awesome—his animal side had a wicked sense of humour and a stubborn determination to do what was right.

She'd been upset at first, she could admit it now, that his bear had stopped the mating from happening. But the inner beast was right. Amber had a part inside her that was distracted from forever, needing to know what had happened to Mason and her parents.

Discovering answers was important. But even more, getting to find out the truth with Cooper at her side—

She rolled with him, her clothing miraculously vanishing before they touched skin to skin. Cooper nibbled the sweet spot under her ear that sent goose bumps flaring in spite of the heat.

Sweet caresses. Touches that scorched her from within and brought need flaring to the surface.

And when Cooper slipped his hips between her legs and lined them up intimately, Amber held his face in her palms and stared into his eyes. Seeing not just the man, and not just the bear, but the whole person. This unique shifter who was *hers*.

Cooper slid home.

He paused, then took her to the pinnacle in long, languid strokes. Each movement concentrated and intense, repeated over and over until he'd pushed them both into blinding pleasure.

The fact that the roof of their snow cave fell in just after they came was somehow the perfect finish. At least once they'd both finished shouting in surprise.

They both found their clothing and dressed rapidly, crawling out of the cave and into the bright but windy day.

Amber made a face as she glanced around. "What a mess. I assume these bumps are the gear I lost when I crashed."

Cooper was already digging equipment free. "It'll take a while to gather it, but we should be okay. As long as the sled starts."

Famous last words.

An hour later they were surrounded by everything they could find, tarps flapping in the strong wind. Amber poked the hunk of metal that was their now-uncooperative sled with her toe. "There goes that plan."

"I guess we have to go to Plan B." There was teasing in his voice.

Stranded in the middle of the wilderness, an icy wind

blowing, and Amber couldn't remember being happier. She grinned at him. "How far away from town are we?"

Cooper checked the GPS he'd managed to dig out of the snow. "Couple of hours, if the weather holds. The wind is actually helping us because it will keep our gear from being covered up again."

Amber nodded briskly. "Then we need to get to town."

He hesitated. "It's a long way to walk. How about if I go first—"

She didn't bother glaring, she just *looked*. "You are not leaving me behind." Besides, if she remembered correctly, his couple of hours to their destination might not be an impossible distance for her.

Cooper didn't argue. "You're right. Sticking together is better. I'll grab us backpacks."

"Wait. I have an idea." She headed to the skid they'd pulled behind the sled and started rummaging through its contents.

"The skidoo is a goner," Cooper said, "Unless you're also a secret mechanic and can MacGyver it back into working order."

"I'm pretty sure I spotted something when we did the transfer..." A sense of satisfaction raced through her as she pulled out a set of skis and the fabric bundle that had been tucked to one side. She held them in the air triumphantly. "Ta-da!"

Cooper sat back on his heels and nodded slowly. "Cross-country skis are better than walking."

She shook the fabric at him. "This is for kite-boarding. Put together *one* backpack, and I'll wear it. Your bear can run with me."

Delight shone on his face. There was approval in his every move as he came over and wrapped her up in a huge hug. "Every time I find out something new about you, it makes me even happier."

The words *I love you* hovered on her lips, but she held back. Just kissed him quickly then hurried to get her gear in place.

It had been a couple of years since she'd donned the equipment, but she'd trust that muscle memory would kick back in. Cooper carefully took off his clothing and tied the bundle onto her pack before helping her into the harness for the kite. "Take a break when you need to," he told her. "Plus you have to keep an eye on the GPS, because my bear's not too good with technology."

She strapped the device on her wrist and checked to make sure she could read it before giving him the go-ahead. "Stay out of my way if I really get trucking," she warned. "It'll take me a while to get warmed up, but I'm sure it's kind of like falling off a bicycle."

Cooper was still chuckling as he shifted, his big bear-self stretching lazily before giving a huge shake. He lifted his gaze.

Amber was weighed down with the backpack, tied into the ropes of her harness. That was the only reason why she didn't slip over to his side to give Cooper the bear a hug.

She truly felt no fear.

Of course, there were no guarantees if he snuck up on her and stuck his big cold nose against her neck. No one should be expected to keep their cool under those circumstances.

She smiled at him, though. "Definitely cute."

He rolled his eyes.

Amber laughed, got her skis lined up properly, and then removed the extra supplies she'd used to pin the parachute fabric of the kite to the ground.

A gust caught the edge of the fabric, lifting it briefly. Amber tugged carefully, and the air currents swooshed in and filled the large rectangle. It angled upward, higher and higher, until the full force of the strong wind took control.

She leaned back in a counterbalance and let herself be pulled forward over the broad field of tundra before her.

For the first five minutes, Amber concentrated on remembering how to work the controls. How to brace her knees as she leaned against the kite's pressure for maximum effect with minimal effort.

When she finally hit that sweet spot—the place where it was as close to flying as she could imagine—she felt comfortable enough to look around.

Cooper was to her right, bounding across the snow with his powerful muscles eating up the distance. For a large animal he moved gracefully, a predator in his home environment.

She could've watched him all day.

Her skis rattled on the ice-crusted snow. The wind pushing her was obviously a familiar part of the terrain, and she set the metal edges of her skis at an angle to aim at the GPS coordinates.

They travelled for nearly an hour before the landscape changed. A series of low hills rose and fell in front of her, and for a moment Cooper vanished from sight.

Amber glanced back to discover he'd slid into position behind her and was now in chase mode. Hot on her heels, Cooper's mouth hung open in an enthusiastic grin. She laughed, turning to check where she was going. The kite tugging on her arms made her shake with effort, but every bit of her felt so alive.

A strange low thumping started in her ears. She glanced to the right as they approached the top of another hill.

Out of nowhere, a helicopter rose into sight. It spun toward them, angling in a high-speed course correction.

Amber tugged the cables controlling her kite to stay out of the helicopter's flight path. It seemed strange that there would be tourists this far north, but perhaps—

The side doors slid open. To her horror, someone braced in the doorway, a long, wicked rifle pointed toward Cooper.

16

*E*verything changed so rapidly, Cooper barely had time to react.

One moment he was having the time of his life, running to the full extent of his bear's strength after Amber. The next moment there was a helicopter, and a flash of light shone down on him that struck him as Not A Good Thing.

Amber's in danger.

He wasn't sure if the thought was his or his bear's. Adrenaline struck, and the instinct to protect was everything. Cooper sprinted toward Amber, trying to get between her and the rapidly approaching vehicle.

He didn't expect her to hit the emergency release on her parachute, coming to an abrupt stop on her skis as the kite fabric fluttered away in the distance like an escaped balloon at a fair.

Amber hit the ground, smacking at her feet as if they were on fire. He'd continued to close the distance between them, attention wavering between the helicopter and her. He wanted to snarl at the intruders. He wanted to rip them apart and keep her safe, but before he could do anything like get in front of her and raise his claws, she popped up and raced across the snow toward him.

She flung her arms around his furry neck, and when she finished swinging, she'd landed as if he were her own personal pony. She grasped his shoulders and spread out, covering as much of his back as her petite body could manage.

"Don't do it," Amber shouted. "Don't you do anything to my bear."

What?

What did she say? Cooper's bear asked in shock.

Busy.

The helicopter landed far enough away to be safe, but close enough that Cooper wanted to curl around Amber to protect her, but she forced his head down and covered his eyes with her hand to protect *him* from the ice crystals driven by the propeller's wind.

As the noise slowly faded, Amber adjusted position and Cooper peeked out from under one paw to discover a couple in drab green uniforms approaching cautiously.

Tranquilizer guns at the ready.

Oh shit.

Cooper didn't move. He'd dealt with this before, and it wasn't much fun.

"Don't shoot. Don't you dare shoot," Amber shouted, waving her arms even as she stayed pressed up against him. "This is my bear, so don't you dare shoot him."

The tips of the guns dipped slightly lower, away from Amber but still possibly targeting Cooper's backside.

"Ma'am?" One of the rangers. The male looked wild-eyed and a lot more unsteady than his female counterpart.

"You point those guns away right now," Amber ordered. "This is my bear, and I do not want you hurting him."

The rangers exchanged glances before the woman turned back to Amber. "Are you sure?"

"Of course, I'm sure. This is my sweet Santa bear. You startled us. We were just out for some exercise."

Something wonderful slid along Cooper's spine, and he rumbled involuntarily with happiness. Amber had dug her fingernails into the itchy space behind his ears, and if she kept it up much longer, he was going to roll on his back and give her his belly, it felt so damn good.

The rangers both made faces, but the woman nodded before turning to her partner. "Go back to the chopper and get it ready. I'll be right there."

"Yes, Caitlin." He marched off, gun still held so he could lift it at a moment's notice if required, glancing over his shoulder again and again to make sure he wasn't going to get pounced on from behind.

Caitlin folded her arms over her uniformed chest and glared at Cooper as Amber got to her feet. "Sweet *Santa* bear? Good grief. I'm amazed my partner fell for it."

Amber hesitated for a moment before shrugging. "He isn't going to hurt me, and that's what it comes down to."

"I'll take your word for that." The ranger eyed Amber. "A polar bear shifter and a human, way out here? You're headed to Bathurst Inlet Settlement, aren't you?"

They were found out.

"How do you know that?" Amber asked.

"It's the only town in the area, and despite your claim you're just out for casual walk, I know you're not local. Besides, I think I know why you've come." Caitlin inclined her head toward the helicopter. "I have to get back. My partner's a human, so I don't mention shifter business around him. The settlement is just over the rise."

She eyed Cooper again.

He stayed very still, the instincts of the predator warning him this was not a moment to act rashly.

Amber stepped forward half a pace, clearly comfortable acting as his protector as she put herself between him and Caitlin. "Thank you for being reasonable."

Caitlin grinned. "Lady, you get points for sheer chutzpah. Safe travels. I'll see you later today."

She turned and walked away, the helicopter propellers beginning their rotation once again.

Amber hid her face against Cooper's neck, staying still until the wind had died down and they were once again alone in the wilderness.

She lifted her head and tugged at his neck. "Well, that was interesting. Let me grab your clothes. It might be safer for both of us to finish the journey on two feet."

Cooper had no objections. He shifted then quickly pulled on his clothes.

"Thank you for the quick thinking," Cooper told her when they were once again headed out, following the GPS beacon. "I was not looking forward to getting tranquilized again."

Amber snorted. "Is this something you do often?"

"Dear God, no." The path was smooth and hard enough to walk on, so Cooper took Amber's gloved hand in his as they paced forward, slow but steady. "Way back when, my brothers and I were playing hide-and-go-seek. Alex and I were a little old for it, but James still loved to play, so we were humouring him. Only, Alex got distracted and took off to investigate some scent trail, and James couldn't find him. Then I got too smart for my own britches and decided to backtrack to keep an eye on James. Make sure he was safe, and all that."

"Of course, you did. He was your little brother," Amber said with a laugh. "I take it you were in bear form?"

"Naturally. I was far enough back I didn't realize he was beginning to panic, and he called nine-one-one because he thought he was lost and so were we."

Amber put her free hand over her mouth, laughter dancing in her eyes.

Cooper sighed dramatically. "The next thing I knew, there was this sharp zap on my butt, then it was like five shots of whiskey flashed through my brain. I woke up in the zoo."

"Oh my God. *Really?*"

"With my parents staring at me through the glass, shaking their heads."

She was still laughing as they crested the low hill. Below them a pretty little village spread nestled against an arm of the Arctic Ocean. Her fingers squeezed tight around his.

Amber took a deep breath, staring up into his eyes. "I have a good feeling about this."

The scent in the air told Cooper there were still adventures to be had. More concerning, though, that electric tingle was back. The one that made it feel as if his skin was getting loose and didn't fit him correctly anymore.

How are you feeling, buddy? he asked his inner bear.

The animal didn't answer for a moment, and when he did, it was slowly, as if deep concentration was involved. *Thinking. Also, this village is full of— Well, this could get uncomfortable. Just a heads-up.*

Cooper had caught the potential trouble. He offered the

beast the equivalent of a bro hug then turned his attention back on Amber.

Her gaze met his straight on. "No matter what happens, I'm with you."

In spite of her positive words, worry filled her eyes, but she stood upright and marched with him down the path leading into town.

Ahead of them, a tall young man stepped out from between two buildings, and a small gasp escaped her.

Cooper tensed, ready to defend her, but Amber was rushing forward with outstretched arms.

"*Mason.*"

The dark-skinned man smiled as he reached for her, twisting slightly to tuck Amber against the side of his body, and held her there with one arm. "It *is* you. Oh, Amber, thank goodness."

Cooper stepped forward, cautious in case his bear riled up at the sight of another man holding her.

Use your brain, the beast drawled. *That's obviously her brother, and considering he's the whole reason we made this trek, I think I can be reasonable.*

Shocking, Cooper teased.

And then he had no more time to taunt his bear because there was too much else going on.

The sound of a child's squall rang out, and Cooper's gaze dropped to the oddly shaped backpack attached to Mason's chest. The reason why he'd hugged Amber to his side.

"Oh. Mason?" Amber stepped back and stared at her brother in shock.

That's when a dark-haired woman with deeply-tanned skin and snapping brown eyes stepped out from the nearest building, and every warning buzzer Cooper had ever received from his shifter side went off.

Damn.

Cooper carefully lowered his gaze, leaning forward so his head was a good foot lower than usual.

The newcomer stepped forward, cocked back a fist and let it fly.

17

*A*mber moved in a rush toward Cooper, shock racing through her between the unexpected discovery of her brother and someone out of the blue clocking her bear smack in the face. "Stop that. What do you think you're doing?"

It was Cooper who held up a hand toward Amber, stepping away from the woman who'd assaulted him. "It's okay. This is standing protocol when our species meet on their turf."

Amber stumbled to a stop, but she nevertheless put herself partially in front of him just in case.

"What does that mean?" She glanced at Mason, who was rocking and bouncing, the sounds of the child going from upset to peaceful once again. "And Mason. It's so good to see you, but a *baby*?"

The first nations woman who'd hit Cooper was now at Mason's side, undoing the ties so she could pull the baby from its carrier.

"Our baby," she said, tucking the child against her chest.

Mason's dark eyes shone with love as he wrapped an arm around the woman's shoulders, embracing the baby as well. He lifted his gaze to Amber's. "It's been a while, and there's a lot to tell, but yes. This is Marianne, and our son is Bram."

The years of not knowing slipped away. She'd had dreams and hopes for her brother, and in one swoop, it seemed they were all answered. Although there were a whole lot of details still missing that needed to be filled in, it was clear Mason was in a place he called home.

The tight knot inside her titled I Don't Know Where He Is But I Hope He's Happy loosened a notch even as emotion rolled her hard. He was safe. He was alive.

He'd never heard of the damn telephone? Or a text message? Or a freaking *postcard*?

Marianne lifted her head and met Amber's eyes. "Come to our house. I guess we have a lot to talk about." She shifted her gaze to Cooper. "Sorry about that."

"No apology needed," Cooper insisted. "Lead the way."

When Mason and Marianne slipped ahead of them, Amber burrowed up against Cooper's side to whisper as softly as possible. "What was that about? Her punching you in the face?"

Cooper whispered back, "This is a village of seal shifters. There've been a few interspecies 'incidents' over the years, and while polar bear shifters now know better, there are some atrocities we need to keep apologizing for."

Polar bears. Seal shifters.

Oh my God. Amber put the two together and came up with a horrible image. "You're kidding me."

"Nope. Thus the standing offer every polar bear gives when meeting members of the seal nation."

And that all made sense now.

They pushed through the door into the cozy home Mason and Marianne led them to. A flurry of activity followed, with other members of the community rushing in to discuss the gear that had been left abandoned on the flats above the valley. Some of them took off on their skidoos to bring it all in.

Fortunately, none of the discussions involved more of the seal clan members punching Cooper in the face. It appeared once was enough per visit.

After quick, refreshing showers, they ended up sitting around the kitchen table, warm soup and biscuits going down easy after the long journey.

Amber and Cooper sat side by side. He had one hand over her thigh and their fingers were tangled together.

She stroked his knuckles even as she turned to Mason. As much as she loved her brother and was thankful to see him, keeping the annoyance out of her voice was impossible. "I've been tracking you for over two years. I would've appreciated if you'd dropped me a line to let me know you were alive."

Mason blinked in surprise. "I sent you updates. Well, more at the beginning than recently, and I wrote because reception was always iffy. You never wrote back, but I figured you were busy, and you knew I was okay." He glanced at Marianne who was spooning soup into Bram's open mouth like he was a little bird. "I was going to call, but then I ended up here and things got complicated."

"Like discovering you were going to be a dad?"

His laughter was soft, his gaze on Marianne tender. "That part came slightly later. First was discovering shifters were a thing. And then fated mates. That was all pretty complicated and not something I could explain in a letter, so I didn't try."

It made a lot of sense. The fact Amber had discovered shifters existed had a lot to do with being in knee-deep with Borealis Gems. "I never got any messages from you."

He looked horrified. "I'm so sorry. I would have tried harder, but I thought—I don't know what I thought."

Wasted time and wasted years, but they were here now, and Amber needed to focus on that. On all the good that was now possible because the mystery had been settled. On the fact she'd never again wake up in the night, heart pounding, imagining the worst.

Never again feel guilty for falling back to sleep after that inexplicable sensation that everything was fine rushed in.

"As it turns out, you could've straight up told me and I would've understood, but there was no way you could've known."

Her brother squeezed her fingers before he leaned in close, eyeing Cooper with suspicion. "I take it he's with you?"

Cooper was staring at Bram, opening and closing his mouth at the same time as the little boy. Amber wasn't sure Cooper was even aware he was doing it.

Her heart gave a huge thump. "He's my mate," she said simply. "We're untangling a few final issues before its official, but yeah. He's with me."

Mason leaned back in his chair and folded his arms over his chest. "Huh. A polar bear shifter. Okay, then. Although it does make for a few complications when it comes to family gatherings."

That was a mouthful.

"It'll be a little interesting, but we'll figure it out," Amber assured him. She hesitated. "Mom and Dad? What did you find?"

His smile increased. "Good news and bad news there. I found them—you're not going to believe this."

"Try me," Amber said dryly. "I can believe a lot these days."

He snorted. "Yeah, I guess. They survived the plane crash, but they're still in recuperation. They're both shifters, which is why the regular search crews didn't find them."

Wow. Unbelievable was right, and yet it made perfect sense.

Amber was going slightly numb with one huge revelation after another, but she managed to speak as if they were having an ordinary, everyday visit. "What kind of shifters, and where are they?"

"Wolverines. They're living with a group of shifters in a remote area of the Yukon. Northern Lights Retreat or something like that. We can Facetime with them if you'd like." He made a face. "Dad still spontaneously shifts at times, which is why they haven't contacted you. Mom figured if you knew they were alive, you'd insist on seeing them, and that really wasn't possible. Now that you know about shifters, I'm sure it'll be okay."

It was a miracle on top of a miracle. "I'm glad to know they're okay. And I'm so happy to have finally found you." She took a deep breath around the knot in her throat. "I missed you."

His eyes sparkled. "I missed you as well. It's good to know you're back in my life."

Amber glanced over at Marianne, checking out this woman who would have been her brother's introduction to the world of shifters and the magical possibilities beyond the human realm. "She's pretty."

"She's perfect," Mason said, adoration in his tone. "She gives me hell when I'm unreasonable, and she makes me laugh, and we just fit. And now that we have Bram, I can't imagine not being with them."

Which was pretty much how she felt about Cooper, and the rest of his family, and her friends in Yellowknife.

As she looked at her brother and his cozy home with his new family, she felt as if her search was complete. He was content, and more than that, he didn't really need her other than as a sister at times. Not the way they'd needed each other growing up.

She took his hand. "I'm glad you found your place. That you found the people you need."

Mason squeezed her fingers back. "I found my heart."

Bram was old enough to sit in a little chair attached to the table, and now that he'd had enough to eat that he wasn't starving, he seemed fascinated by Cooper's fingers.

Cooper and Marianne had been talking quietly about fishing and other shifter-type topics while she fed Bram. Cooper had stretched his free arm out within reach of Amber's nephew, and now every time Bram reached for one of his big fingers, Cooper would wiggle it slightly and send the little boy into gales of laughter.

Amber's heart turned to mush at the sight of her big bear and the little baby.

Marianne was slowly losing her stiffness, and she turned and offered Amber a true smile. "We don't have room here, but my parents' cottage is open for you to use. They went south to visit my sisters. Tomorrow is Christmas Eve, and I hope you'll stay to celebrate with us."

Amber had totally lost track of time over the course of

the past week. "I had no idea we'd hit the holidays. If it won't put you out, we'd love to stay."

"You're family," Marianne said. "It's never going to be a problem for you to visit."

Cooper was sitting motionless. Bram had his fingers wrapped in a death grip around Cooper's thumb, and it looked as if her big polar bear was content to sit there until he was let free.

Amber slid her arm around Cooper and squeezed tight as she answered for them. "Then we'd love to. Thank you."

They visited longer, including a video chat with Amber's parents, which set her crying a little. She clung to Cooper's hand even as she wiped away the tears. They laughed together at shared memories and when her dad accidentally shifted back and forth between fur and human a couple of times, no one so much as blinked.

After dinner they were given a tour of town then guided to their promised cottage.

Mason invited them to come back to his home after they'd gotten settled, but Amber shook her head. She wanted to visit with him and his family, but not now.

It was already late, and someone else in the room needed her attention.

"I'm glad we found you, Mason. And I'm even happier to see how much this is your home. But can we catch up tomorrow? It's been a big day after a lot of other big days."

"Of course." Mason squeezed her tight in one of those hugs she remembered so well from her growing-up days. A hug that said she was important to him. "We'll spend time together in lots of tomorrows."

She closed the door behind him and turned to face her big polar bear. After the rush of all sorts of emotions—the joy and shock and amazement of finding Mason and her parents—through it all, she'd been utterly aware of Cooper.

Now as she walked across the simple cottage-like space toward him, it was with so much love inside her wanting to burst free. She held it back, though, sensing he needed something.

"What's wrong?" she asked.

He led her to the couch and sat, their hands linked, a frown creasing between his brows. "I'm not sure—"

Cooper shook his head as if chasing away flies then, his eyes widening, he slipped away and stripped his shirt off over his head.

Okay. She kinda thought they were going to talk first but...

Cooper grinned even as he undid his pants and stepped out of them, getting naked. "This is most definitely a first, but I have been ordered to shift. I'm not sure why, but this time, I don't think I should argue."

Amber was going to ask for further explanation, but she wasn't going to get any because Cooper was already shifting. The man vanished and the bear arrived, sitting on the hearthstones in the small living space that was barely big enough for him to turn around in.

When he padded forward and laid his chin on her knee, Amber gave in and ran her fingers through his fur, petting him. "Thank you for everything you did to get me here."

It was a good thing she was sitting down, because the next thing she heard was very clearly Cooper's voice. Only it wasn't quite Cooper, and she wasn't hearing it with her ears.

The voice sounded in her head.

"You did so much to make the trip successful. You're good for Cooper, and I see now you'll be good for me as well."

Amber let out an unsteady breath and tried to answer back. *"Cooper?"*

"Yes... And no. I don't think he can hear you because he's not talking to you. I am."

Cooper had once said that it was complicated, the relationship between him and his bear. Man, he wasn't kidding. *"Okay. So, while I have a chance, do you know that I think you're marvelous?"*

The bear swung a paw gently, as if batting away a butterfly. *"You really are a sweet talker, but I kind of like that. You can tell me nice things anytime you want. And the scratching behind the ears is very acceptable, as well."*

"I'll remember that." Amusement and excitement were bubbling together inside Amber's gut, and she wanted to be able to talk to Cooper about this, but she didn't want this experience to end, either. *"Does this mean Cooper and I are mates? I mean, this really is complicated, talking about you and Cooper as if you're two different people, but are you okay with me being in your life?"*

In her lap, the bear's head dipped. *"First, though, I need to apologize."*

Amber waited because there was obviously more coming.

She swore the bear swallowed hard before he continued. *"I told Cooper there would be no mating until you had room for me. That was wrong. I thought that looking for your brother meant you had a missing place inside. But I heard you talk with Mason. I sense how much you care for him, and your parents, but your first touch is always for Cooper. For me. And your friends. Now I understand that you can care for more people without dividing love. Love is not a finite amount, it's something that grows. Expands to fill the space..."*

It was a difficult concept, and yet the simplest thing in the world.

Maybe, just maybe, it was also the reason she'd never given up hope. Never truly felt abandoned or alone. She'd *had* love with her all the days of her journey. Hope and love and optimism were as natural to her as breathing, or as...

As natural as shifting was to a certain bear of her heart.

"I can love my brother, and my friend Kaylee, and all of Cooper's family, and my new sister-in-law and nephew, and I will still have room to love Cooper and you, his inner bear, with everything in me. Because love does grow."

"This is a good thing," Cooper's bear informed her.

Moisture filled her eyes. Happy tears. *"It's a very good thing."*

"I'll tell Cooper to shift back, and then you can have fun. But remember the ear scratching. And the compliments. I'll remind you if you forget."

She was laughing as the conversation cut out and Cooper shifted back into a naked man, now kneeling between her thighs.

He wore a slightly puzzled expression. "That was the most bizarre sensation."

Amber cupped his face in her hand. "Did you hear us?"

Cooper shook his head. "Nothing more than that sound you hear in the Peanuts movies when the adults are talking. Blah, blah, blah."

Interesting. Amber did her best to try and talk to him the way she'd been speaking with his bear. *"Can you hear this?"*

"I can, he can't."

Cooper blinked hard. "You just did it again. What's going on?"

Amber thought it through then answered slowly. "It

appears I can talk to your bear, and he can talk to me, and while that's all fascinating, I think the most important part to tell you is that he no longer objects to our mating."

Joy lit his expression. "That's great." He stopped. "Then why aren't we mated?"

18

*A*n absolute swing of emotions had rolled up one side of Cooper and down the other.

He'd never had his bear take charge like that before, but it had definitely been an order when he'd been told to shift. It had worried him for a moment—with Alex's warnings and all—then his bear had added an unexpected *please*.

The command wasn't a bear rebellion, but a sweet and heartfelt plea, and suddenly the last thing Cooper had been worried about was being hoodwinked by his inner beast.

Obviously something had happened between Amber and his bear that went far beyond the normal.

But now Amber was sitting there, after giving him the best news he'd heard in a long time, seemingly unfazed by the fact that nothing big and wild had happened.

Instead, she shrugged. "I don't know why nothing seems to have changed. Time delay? What's supposed to happen when we're officially mates?"

"I was thinking more along the lines of the whole wildness that happened with Kaylee and James back at the start of summer. You know, the tornado-on-the-stage kind of thing."

Amber looked thoughtful. "But Lara told me that with her and Alex, it wasn't until he bit her, in that way that wolves do, that everything went through for them."

"Alex told me the same thing." This just got more and more confusing. "Hang on. Let me check something."

You there?

Not sure where exactly you thought I might go, but yes.

Everyone was a comedian today. *So, you're okay if Amber and I are mates?*

Pretty sure that's what I told her. You should listen to her a little better, considering you're going to be stuck with each other from now till forever.

You're particularly snarky tonight. How about constructive suggestions as to why nothing very shifter-like has happened, since you're no longer objecting?

He got a pause this time then an internal shrug. *Must have something to do with human traditions. Can't help you there. Although if you want to mention something important to Amber?*

Yes?

Tell her I'm particularly fond of compliments regarding my athletic prowess.

The urge to tell his bear to stop flirting with his woman was far too weird, and Cooper filed that away under Wild Shit That Happens To Shifters Who Mate Humans.

He met Amber's gaze. "The only thing he suggests is completing some human tradition." Sudden terror struck. "Don't tell me you want to have a big wedding. I mean, *do* tell me if you want to have a big wedding, but—"

Panic was not a sensation he was familiar with, but it was easily recognizable. Tension swirled in his gut, and bright lights flashed behind his eyes as if he were one step away from fainting.

Settle down, his bear said with a laugh. *If she wants to do the big wedding thing, we can survive.*

These things take time, Cooper warned. *I would prefer to be permanently hitched sooner than later. That's all.*

Sure. I believe you. His inner beast's tone was mocking. Extremely mocking. *Mr. We Should Wait Until The Appropriate Time.*

There was that staticky buzz in his head again, and Amber's eyes widened. Was his bear chatting with her?

I wish you'd find a way to loop me in, Cooper complained.

Busy talking. Don't interrupt the grown-ups.

Cooper sputtered.

Amber snorted, hard, then flushed. "He's very vocal, isn't he? Your inner bear."

"He's a pain in the tuchus, is what he is," Cooper grumbled before it registered that he was down on his knees in front of her and maybe this was part of what he could do to trigger their own special mating. "Amber?"

She smiled sweetly. "Yes?"

He slid his hands under hers, lifting her knuckles to his lips for a brief kiss. He stared into her eyes and let every bit of the love he felt for her shine.

One more deep breath, and it was time. "Will you be my mate?"

She blinked hard, her expression brightening as awareness quickly arrived. Her smile softened, eyes filling with moisture. "Yes."

They waited.

Like statues. Neither of them breathed or looked away...

The walls of the cabin creaked with the intense cold outside, and a log crackled in the fireplace. Nothing else.

Clearly nothing magical was about to sweep into the room and whirl around them.

Amber wrinkled her nose in the most adorable way. "Okay, so that wasn't it."

"I guess not." He pulled her forward and wrapped his arms around her, cradling her intimately. "I'm still glad the answer was yes. And you're right. We'll figure it out, if it's a time delay or something else. We'll do it together."

"Yes, we will." Amber slid her cheek alongside of his, squeezing him tight. A sharp nip at his ear sent a shiver sliding down his spine, especially when it was followed by a slow lick, her tongue hot and wet against his skin. "It seems a pity to waste you being naked, and all. There's a warm fire, and a soft rug..."

A delicious woman for him to enjoy from top to bottom. "I like the way you think, Amber Myawayan."

He also liked the way she tasted, the way she kissed, and the way she moaned his name when he made her come. It was a most entertaining evening.

Darkness still covered the village when they woke. Cooper stoked the fire then crawled back into bed, happy for the mattress after their time spent roughing it.

He played with Amber's hair, stroking it through his fingers as she stared sleepily at him, a contented expression on her face. "We'll have to figure out a way to get home, but we can stay and visit for as long as you'd like."

"I don't want to keep you from your family for too long," Amber told him. "Plus, I think I'll be coming to visit often."

"We can definitely put that in a plan."

She laughed, then her expression grew serious. "I need to tell you something."

Cooper tensed.

Even with Amber flat on the mattress, it looked as if she steeled her spine. "When I came to your hideout for mating fever, I told you I was on birth control. I am... or was. It's out there somewhere in a snowbank. Which means I should've thought of it sooner. Before we had sex last night."

Interesting development.

"I'm not too worried," Cooper admitted. "Number one because I don't think you missing a day or so would set you ovulating right away. But now I have a question for you, as I refer back to our mating fever discussions and one of the differences between us." He stretched beside her, resting his head on an arm. "You're young. We never talked about if you want kids. Or if you do want them, how long you want to wait before we start."

She got that look about her. The one meaning that while she was embarrassed, she wasn't about to let this opportunity slip past. "I want kids, and I'm interested in having them whenever it happens." She damn near fluttered her lashes at him. "Seeing little Bram yesterday made me realize that. But it was seeing you with him—good grief, I may have gotten pregnant right then and there because my ovaries went into overdrive."

Cooper laughed. The sound broke free, impossible to stop. She was so serious yet so sweetly intense in that way she got when she talked with her friends, and what he felt inside welled up and over, deeper and richer. "Then we won't worry about missed birth control pills, because I'm good with whenever it happens, as well."

Then, because it seemed appropriate, he rolled her on top of him and encouraged her to wake up all the way, as enthusiastically as she liked.

It was nearly noon before they made it out of the

cottage, stepping carefully on the snowy footpaths back to Mason's house.

Ahead there was a clatter of voices, and Cooper kept a firm grip on Amber's hand as he diverted them toward a new location.

Overhead, a plane buzzed as it circled the community, the reason for the gathering now clear. People had gathered at the edge of the airstrip on the outskirts of the community.

Cooper chuckled as he realized Amber had moved in front of him as if to protect him.

And he'd let her.

She glanced over her shoulder, blinked, then grinned.

The plane landed and slowly taxied toward the gathering, and as he recognized the vehicle, the place inside Cooper that was full of love for his family lit up again.

"Oh my goodness. *Really?*" Amber said a moment before the plane stopped and the side hatch swung open. Family and friends poured out to the ground, Kaylee and Lara glancing around eagerly.

A moment later, the three women were tangled in a hug.

Alex descended a little slower, his hands full of bags. James paced after him. Both of them dropped their loads to the ground and held up their arms so they could make cheering motions toward Cooper.

Alex hesitated, glancing toward James as two women in the crowd stepped forward.

The brothers quickly bent their knees and leaned lower, heads snapping back in unison as fists made brisk contact.

A second later, they'd all moved on. The woman who had punched Alex patted him on the back before pushing him toward his mate. It was Caitlin, their ranger from the previous day. The woman was also a seal shifter, which explained so much.

"Remind her not to tear my head off, will you, Amber?" Caitlin asked with a dash of amusement.

Amber had been restraining Lara and offered a quick thumbs-up.

Yup. Visits to Amber's brother were going to be entertaining, that was for sure.

"What are you doing here?" Cooper asked as his brothers rubbed their hands briskly over their jaws.

"We came to celebrate the holidays with you, of course." James shrugged. "Not much use in having a pilot in the family if you don't take advantage of it."

"When we got the word you'd arrived and Amber had found her brother, we were all pretty excited," Alex said. "Gramps insisted we come and join you so it could be a real family celebration."

Of course the old man had insisted. The meddlesome, conniving man had been doing everything in his power to get Cooper hooked up with Amber. Bless his heart, in the good way.

A sudden clatter rang out from behind them, and the bottom panel fell out of the plane. Three lanky figures tumbled to the ground with shouts and groans.

Lara pinched the bridge of her nose before planting both fists on her hips and glaring at the stowaways. "Seriously, dudes? In what universe did you think this was a good idea?"

They all popped to their feet, Dixon's familiar face in their midst. He stepped forward, still brushing snow off his pants. "Heard you were going on a bit of an adventure. Thought you might need some backup." He turned toward

Amber and grinned hugely. "We're *totally* building you that statue. You rock. So hard."

Nothing but amusement bubbled up from his bear side, which Cooper was grateful for. He ignored the wolves because they were Lara and Alex's problem.

Instead, he slapped a hand on his brothers' shoulders. "I'm glad you're here." He turned to where Mason and Marianne were waiting at the edge of the gathering, offering them a huge smile. "It's time to get ready for that celebration. Put us to work."

19

As parties went, the day rated right up there as one of Amber's best memories.

Not only did she have Cooper at her side, she had her best friends, Lara and Kaylee. There were Mason and his wife to rekindle memories with and build new ones.

Their small house was filled to the brim when you added James and Alex, *and* Dixon and his friends.

Little Bram looked around with wide eyes, lifting his hands with imperial dignity as he demanded to be passed from person to person for hugs and cuddles. Dixon turned out to love kids, and eventually it was the two of them—the enthusiastic wolf and the nearly-a-toddler, ensconced together in a corner of the house where childish laughter rang out over and over, bringing smiles to everyone's faces as they worked.

"You've been so good to open your home to us," Amber said to Mason in the middle of one of the calmer moments.

"You're a miracle worker for finding enough food to feed us all," Cooper added.

"That was all Marianne." Mason glanced at his mate, that tender expression in his eyes flashing again. "And the rest of the clan. I hope you like fish."

"You don't even have to cook it," Amber teased, dancing out of Cooper's reach.

The entire day was like that. Little bursts of conversation, time spent with her friends. A sweet moment post-lunch when she cuddled with Bram as he grew heavy-lidded then fell asleep on her with complete trust.

Amber didn't move. Just stared down at the beautiful child in her arms and let deliciously happy thoughts drift through her brain.

A big set of arms wrapped around her, and another layer of delight arrived like icing on the cake.

"Hey, Cooper."

"Hey, darling. How's your holiday going?"

She gazed into his eyes. They still hadn't experienced whatever mystical magic needed to occur for the mating *woo-woo*, but she had faith it would happen when it was supposed to.

But *this* was supposed to happen right now. She used her free arm to catch Cooper around the neck, tugging him toward her so he could kiss her.

The catcalls were quiet to avoid waking the sleeping baby.

At different moments, couples vanished then returned, taking time to stretch their legs or return to their rooms to nap. The sun was only out for a short period of time, and everyone made sure to go outside and enjoy the brief blast as it rose just in line with the horizon.

The day vanished, and so did the food that had been on the dinner table, causing it to groan under the weight. Bears and wolves and seals all ate until the bountiful spread was nearly vanished. Then they pushed back their chairs, hands falling over stomachs that were just a little too full.

"I wish I hadn't finished that last piece of pie," Dixon said gloomily.

Alex nodded at the young man. "You're learning. Overindulgence is sometimes a mistake."

Dixon blinked. "I didn't mean I wouldn't eat it. I'm just regretting that the pecan pie is gone—that was the last piece. Now I have to go find my second favourite."

He bounced to his feet amazingly quickly considering the amount of food he'd consumed. Laughter swelled again, and it was...right.

It was family. Amber leaned on Cooper's arm and soaked it all in.

The dishes were stacked and brought to the kitchen, and after a whirlwind of activity, the house was clean and the living space had been transformed.

Amber wasn't sure whose eyes were wider, Bram's or Dixon's.

A stack of presents had appeared out of nowhere. Brightly coloured with ribbons and bows sparkling in the reflected lights on the Christmas tree.

Kaylee settled beside Amber. "Grandpa was delighted to surprise us with the trip here. Then imagine what our faces must've looked like when Grandma pulled out two Santa-sized sacks of goodies."

"We decided to haul everything we had wrapped up along for the ride," Lara confessed, cuddling in tighter under Alex's arm. "It does look as if we held up the North Pole, doesn't it?"

"As long as you didn't import any elves, we're okay."

Mason reached into the massive stack and without reading the name, tossed the first gift to Amber. "Merry Christmas, sis."

The couch dipped heavily as Cooper settled on her other side. As the presents continued to be handed out all around her, Amber paused to read the card on her gift.

Looking forward to making new memories with you.
—Mason

It was a book full of drawings. Sketches Mason had made along the route he'd travelled in search of their parents. During the years apart, she'd wondered what he'd been doing and what he'd been seeing—she now had a record of the places and the people who were meaningful during that time.

It was telling that the most recent pictures included a lot of Marianne, and the final pages, Bram.

She held the book to her chest and looked across the chaos of the room to where her brother sat with his family. He was smiling at her. That smile that went all the way to his eyes.

He mouthed *I love you* and she said it back.

Then she brushed away a tear and tried to catch up on exactly who had gotten what, but never quite figured out why Dixon had a duck on his head.

There were some mysteries that would never be solved.

Cooper was staring at something in his hand.

"What did you get?" Amber asked.

"You'll find out soon enough." He carefully folded and tucked the whatever-it-was into the pocket of his shirt without letting her see, which she thought was kind of mean. But he squeezed her tight and gave her the most delicious kiss, which mostly made up for it.

A sudden bang hit the door, and everyone turned to discover Kaylee and James peeking into the room. They were wearing all their winter gear, and Kaylee's cheeks were rosy from the cold. She also looked a little tumbled, and Amber figured she and James must have snuck outside to fool around.

"You guys. The sky is amazing right now. Everybody's *got* to see it," Kaylee insisted.

There was a rush to find winter clothing, but eventually everyone poured outside, climbing the small hill behind Mason's house to get away from the streetlights. They all stared up at a light show bigger than any Amber had ever seen before.

From one side of the horizon to the other, streaks of blue, green, indigo, and violet danced and wove and slid as if a hand was wiping paint across an enormous canvas. Amber tucked her fingers into Cooper's and kept her gaze fixed on the heavens. Complete awe left her speechless.

At least until he squeezed her fingers and she turned to face him. The lights continued to dance like a halo around his head, reflecting in his eyes and shining off the silver flecks in his hair.

The words came now.

"I love you." Amber cupped his face with her hand, and he leaned against it. "I really do," she admitted. "Even if it seems fast, it isn't. I've been falling in love with you for the past two years, and now there's just so much of it inside me that there's nowhere for it to go except all over you."

Cooper's face split into an enormous grin. "You're so perfect. And somehow you've managed to jump the gun every single time I try to surprise you."

Amber paused for a moment, not sure what that meant.

Cooper dropped to one knee and pulled out a ring case, holding it up to her. "Amber Myawayan, I love you too. Will you be my forever, however that looks?"

Oh my goodness. The lights were everywhere overhead, and a slow shimmer seemed to sink into her bones as if the snow were glowing, and all she could see was that love in his eyes. It was true, and it was truth, and it was everything she ever needed.

She leaned in closer. "I will be yours. You will be mine. All of you, by the way. Now and forever."

He slipped the ring on her finger then pulled her toward him, kissing her firmly. Sealing the deal, as it were.

A terrible, wonderful idea sprang to mind. Amber took a quick glance around. They were on the very edge of the gathering, darkness all around them. Most people were wandering toward the house, where Mason was bringing out lawn chairs for watching the light show.

Amber pulled Cooper to his feet and tugged him in the opposite direction.

"What are we doing?" he asked.

"You'll find out soon enough," she said with a tease.

Once they were out of earshot of the gathering, Amber gave him no warning. She leapt into his arms and grabbed hold of both sides of his jacket, unzipping it in one motion then reaching for his belt.

Cooper didn't need any further explanations.

It was a good thing he was a shifter and used to getting rid of clothing in a hurry.

It was a better thing he was a shifter and his body temperature was well above hers as a human, because by the time she was partially naked, she was wondering if her idea was really such a good one.

Except he pulled her onto the nest he'd made from the discarded clothing. Tucked away from the wind, with his big chest acting as a radiator, she was toasty warm as he used his hands to heat her up in the best way possible.

Cooper nibbled on the spot on her neck that drove her wild. "I love you so much," he whispered.

She swore she heard a rush of music sweep across the sky with another spectacular burst of dancing lights. Cooper's hands danced over her skin, lights reflected everywhere, and he drove her quickly to the point of no return. Hesitated, and then slid home.

If anything, the lights only got brighter. There were explosions and swirling fireworks, and all of it was part of nature and all of it was perfect.

Cooper moved them together, bringing them up and then letting them fly.

Magic arrived in a way Amber had never experienced before.

It wasn't just the physical pleasure. It wasn't just the love in Cooper's eyes. The spectacular aurora borealis dancing over their heads and bathing their bodies with shimmering light was part of it, and the fact that they were here, her and Cooper, individuals, a pair, and yet a part of a huge whole called family—

There was magic in that moment, and they both knew it.

Cooper swore, soft and reverent, because something beautiful had just happened.

Amber's heart was still pounding from the sex, but as she lay cradled in Cooper's arms, something else was there. A connection that was 100 percent happiness and wonder.

Cooper stared at her in amazement. "Amber? Do you feel that?"

They were one. The sensation was brand-new and in an even more intimate way than the physical joining of sex.

"Does this mean we're mates for real?" she asked.

He pressed a kiss to her lips. "We are. Forever."

20

*T*hey stayed in the settlement until the day after Boxing Day.

It was just after lunch when they gathered by the plane, two separate parties preparing to take off in different directions.

Alex and Lara had decided to take her wolves and a sled and do the journey in reverse to gather any supplies Cooper and Amber had abandoned on the trip north. Traveling with four of them in wolf or bear form, and one in human meant they could take turns and complete the trip in only a few days.

Alex grinned at Cooper when he paced over to say farewell. "Lara got a straight answer out of Dixon. He came up with the stowaway gig because the couple of guys with him don't do well without Alpha supervision. There was talk of over-the-top mischief. Lara is going to run the rebellion out of them."

"Makes sense." Cooper frowned. "But now I'm curious. Who *has* been in charge while you and Lara were here?"

"Auntie Amethyst," Alex said with a laugh. "She was

delighted to do it. Other than a few problem children, I'm sure she's having the time of her life bossing them all around."

Cooper could see that. "Thanks for grabbing our stuff."

His brother examined him carefully. "You seem solid. How's the situation between you and Amber?"

"Great. It's not exactly what I expected, but there's something uniquely ours about this mating."

Alex hesitated. "And your bear is fine?"

Good grief. "He's never been better. He's constantly taunting me with the fact he can talk to Amber, and I can't."

"That's so weird," Alex said. "But like you said, it seems to be just how it works for you two."

Cooper wrapped Alex in a huge bro hug, pounding between his shoulder blades firmly before letting him go. "We'll see you back in Yellowknife." Then he caught Amber up in his arms and carried her to the plane, her laughing eyes his strongest memory from the journey home.

Now it was New Year's Eve, and the entire family had gathered at Grandmother and Grandfather's for the dual celebration. They would ring in the new year as a family, but they were also toasting Grandfather's eighty-fifth birthday.

Giles Borealis sat at the head of the table, glass of whiskey beside him and a contented smile on his face. "You've done me proud, boys. Never dreamed what a blessing it would be to have this day come. You've more than made this old man happy, and you deserve every bit of goodness coming your way."

He indicated the slim envelopes beside each of their plates, which Cooper assumed contained the specifics of the new ownership of Borealis Gems. He really didn't need to open it right now.

He already had the biggest reward in his life—his mate.

Alex's phone went off as a Facetime call came in from their parents, and the whole family gathered around to talk to Giles Jr. and Glenda Borealis. Gentle teases and excited good wishes were all part of it.

Cooper stepped back and let his brothers do the majority of the talking.

When the visit was over, he glanced across the room and discovered his grandmother smiling at him with approval.

He went and pressed a kiss to her cheek. "I love you, Gram."

"I love you too, sweetie."

Everyone else in the room was still busy chatting, and it felt appropriate to ask, all things considered. "You sent me the ring for Amber, didn't you? I thought I recognized it."

Grandma Laureen nodded, her soft smile shining on her face. "I wasn't sure your mating would go exactly the way it did with Giles and myself, but having the support of family made a difference. Plus, a ring is a human bit of tradition, and I wasn't sure you'd remember that little detail."

He'd never even thought about his grandparents' mating other than knowing that humans and polar bears could successfully be together for a long time. "Grandma, not to be impolite, but can you and Grandfather talk to each other like mated shifters?"

She glanced across the room, her bright gaze dancing over his grandfather. Giles was laughing with Amber as she tried unsuccessfully to blow out what had to be a trick candle on his cake.

Suddenly Grandfather Giles looked up, turning his attention toward his mate then fixing a stare on Cooper.

"Don't know why you never asked me," he shouted across the distance. "Young whippersnappers."

Which answered that question. Sort of.

Grandma Laureen raised a brow. "We have our ways," she said mysteriously.

Suspicion rose as he eyed her back. "That wasn't an answer."

"You're smart enough to figure it out," she said with a wink. Then she rose and joined Kaylee and Lara, who were pulling out a box from behind the couch.

Oh.

Oh.

Could you tell Amber I'd like to play a trick on my grandfather? Cooper said to his bear.

I don't know if I want to be your delivery boy, his inner bear teased good-naturedly. *Except, when I chat with Amber, she says nice things to me. So... Okay. What's the message for our gal?*

Stop flirting with my mate, Cooper said.

Our mate. What's the trick?

Tell her to ask him if he still has that bottle of Macallan Estate single malt whiskey hidden behind the antique set of encyclopedias. And if he does, the boys would love a drink.

The now-familiar buzzing went off at the back of his brain. It wasn't uncomfortable. In fact, it was soothing to know that his bear was in love with Amber as well and wanted the best for her.

When his grandfather went into a coughing spree on the other side of the room, Cooper turned his back to hide his grin.

Amber says he wants to know how she knows about that.

She also knows about the smoked-salmon stash in the game room fridge. He should just break out the liquor, or she'll also know about the Ghirardelli in the freezer that Grandmother would simply love.

This time the buzzing came at the same time as his bear's response, which made Cooper suspect the beast had figured out how to talk to both of them at the same time. *I like you being devious. Also, did you mention smoked salmon?*

You're a good bear. I'll save some for you to enjoy tonight on our walk.

I like you, dude. We're a good team.

A few minutes later Amber was beside him, her face glowing and a brimming glass of whiskey in her hand. "Your grandfather sent this with his compliments and a request that you not tell me all his secrets. He seems to think I might tell your grandmother."

"Because you would, wouldn't you, dear?" Grandmother Laureen waved them over, the Ghirardelli chocolate bar in her fingers wiggling like a flag.

Cooper kissed Amber. Carefully, because of the fifty-year-old whiskey in one hand.

She led him to where their family were waiting eagerly. Lara held out a brightly wrapped present. Two more rested at Kaylee's and Lara's feet.

Amber frowned. "Christmas is over."

"I forgot to put these in the bags we sent earlier," Grandmother Laureen explained. "They're just something fun."

By now everyone was gathered in the living room. Alex sat on the arm of Lara's chair. James and Kaylee were on the floor, side by side, legs tangled together.

Grandfather was in his easy chair, Grandmother next to him. They held hands over the short distance between them, the connection as tight as if they were one person.

Cooper noticed all this in a moment as he took in the room and the people in his heart who were near.

He settled Amber on the couch beside him, his arm wrapped around her, but knew that if they'd been sitting on opposite sides of the room, they'd feel just as close.

Amber tore into her gift's wrapping paper as Lara and Kaylee did the same. Glittering blue and green and gold metallic shreds flew through the air like a miniature aurora had taken over the room.

"He's so cute." Lara lifted a stuffed wolf from the box. She turned to Alex and made it growl at him. "Snarl and snarl and *grrrrr*."

"I got a bobcat," Kaylee exclaimed. She placed the pillow-sized creature on James's lap and pretended to scratch it behind the ears. "She's adorable. Thank you, Grandmother."

Cooper was holding his breath. His grandmother's eyes danced with mischief.

Amber pulled out a stuffed polar bear. Incredibly soft, the little thing had big blue eyes and a sweet heart-shaped nose, and when Amber held it in her arms, Cooper just about fell off the couch.

She looks good with a baby. Is that what you just said? His inner bear demanded rather vigorously. *Did you say baby?*

Hush, Cooper warned.

Oh, hell no. Not being quiet. Are you not telling me something? His bear paused. *Wait. Why am I asking you?*

Don't—

It was too late. His bear was talking with Amber and her cheeks grew even more heated, and her eyes were dancing more than Grandmother's.

He ignored the family in the room and took Amber's

face in his hands. Staring into her eyes as he poured out the truth. "I love you. Now and forever. All of you, with all of me."

She smiled then, just for him. "I love you too."

Amber turned back to the rest of the family and thanked Grandmother sweetly.

Becoming A Mate To His Perfect Woman was already the best thing that had happened to him. Cooper held her, and the stuffed polar bear, and decided if Becoming A Family was in his near future, life would be just fine.

Because he'd be doing it all with his forever mate.

EPILOGUE

Personal Journal, Giles Borealis, Sr.

S atisfaction.

Oh, I could call it pride, or accomplishment, but no matter how well my plans worked, the truth is at this point of the game, the only thing that matters is that my grandchildren are all healthy, happy, and mated.

I'm fairly certain that great-grandbabies are on the way, as well, but I'll let the boys share that detail in their own sweet time. No need for me to pry into those details.

Yet.

Not that I ever intrude where I'm not wanted, mind you. Only offer wise and gentle suggestions to nudge those who need a little help toward their proper place full of happiness.

Today was the culmination of so many plans. After sending the children north for Christmas, it was only right that they come and spend the day with us. It was my birthday, after all.

Seeing the three couples together showed me how perfect each pair is for each other, and yet so different.

James and Kaylee are still best friends, but now the love between them glows brighter than our namesake. She's learning that her value isn't based on being loud or outspoken, but on being her own unique self. While her human side will never be the star of any social event, her sweet confidence is building as James loves her unconditionally.

Glad that all those years ago, Kaylee's parents and our children ended up living next door to each other. That coincidence allowed this particular romance to set some roots. Friends as children, forever as adults.

Although they're still playful like children in some ways. Kaylee's bobcat jumped into the middle of a wolf pack brawl the other day—oh, the laughter from the boys at her boldness, and the utter shock on those lupine faces...

Have to admit I never dreamed one of my kin would end up involved in a wolf pack—a wolf pack!—or mated to the Alpha, but Alex is the perfect consort to Lara. She leads that unruly mob with power and wisdom, and he's there to support and care for her. Just the way a mate should.

And if they still have the occasional fight or two, well, that's the hot-blooded Borealis in him and the unbreakable Lazuli spirit in her, and a few heated tussles are good for keeping warm in these northern climes.

He was a little wide-eyed when he came to me on the sly and admitted they don't always agree about everything. I assured him that his grandmother and I butt heads to this very day. But we never go to bed without making up, so I informed Alex, and he agreed it was a good habit to build.

Glad that girl decided to return to the north where I could make sure they butted heads until their hearts got involved.

And finally Cooper. The boy wanders around wearing

an expression of astonishment. He's rightly amazed at the perfect partner he's found in Amber. Have to admit that girl surprised me a little. I did what I could to push them in the right direction—only a nudge or two, because I don't like to meddle.

But it was all her skills and bravery—including standing up to the stubbornness of a polar bear—that made the final decision. She's going to be one hell of a partner for him. Just like he's the only one who's perfect to help her in the future. A part of Borealis Gems, a part of the Borealis family. Starting their own family...

Yes, I have my suspicions, but in their own good time...

Next week would be fine.

In the meanwhile, I have new plans to make, new plots to tangle. My birthday may be over, but there's a special anniversary coming up soon with the only woman who ever had a chance at my heart and soul.

Working on forever with a mate is about as perfect as life can get, which is why I wanted this for my grandsons.

I know what love brings to a man. I cherish it every day, along with my Laureen's sweet, giving heart. I don't know what I'd do without her. Good thing I don't have to find out. Mates are forever, and that's exactly what I want.

Forever with her.

EPILOGUE

*L*aureen Borealis shook her head at the light still shining at the top of the stairs.

"He's gone and left the lights on again. 'I never leave the lights on, my love,'" she grumbled in imitation of Giles. "That's what the man would tell me, but there's the proof."

She smiled, though, as she made her way up the wide steps toward her husband's den. The rich wood interior fit his style, welcoming and comfortable at the same time.

Maybe too comfortable—

Giles was behind his desk, but he wasn't working. Feet on the desk, head tilted back, a smile on his lips. Snoring softly with his hands folded over his chest. He clutched his wedding ring tightly as if protecting it.

Powerful love bloomed yet again, the way it had every day since he'd walked into her life nearly sixty years ago. Her mate—her heart.

Her everything.

Laureen moved carefully to avoid waking him, tidying the glass and bowl on the desk top—

His journal lay open. His rich script was like artwork, and she drew closer to admire his neatly formed characters and perfect syntax...

Okay, fine. She was being nosy and wanted to see what he'd written. He'd long ago given her permission to snoop, saying he would never keep any real secrets from the woman he loved more than life itself.

He'd admitted he liked that she wanted to see and understand the most intimate part of him—his thoughts.

It only took a moment to skim through the most recent entry, and by the time she was done, her smile was wider and her heart even more full. Seeing what he'd been doing in the background to create the perfect setups for each of their grandsons had been entertaining.

Giles hadn't been the least bit modest—not that she ever expected him to be anything but boastful in his own private journal. A fantastic salute to his successful meddling and manipulations.

He'd done well, and she was proud of him. Although...

His conniving wasn't *all* the truth, but he didn't know that.

Oh, he *had* done a lot. Planned and plotted and made suggestions and pulled strings at what seemed to be pivotal moments.

She couldn't have done it without him.

Her lips twitched with amusement.

She'd done her own plotting and planning, starting long before last Christmas. That's when she'd finally decided everything was in place.

She could still remember the conversation they'd had after the family had left. The presents all unwrapped, the farewells and well-wishes sent after their son and daughter-in-law as Giles Jr. and Glenda left the country and placed the grandsons in charge...

She and Giles had settled by the fire, a glass of wine for her, a whiskey for him.

"Family visits are the best." Giles sighed heavily, contentment in his tone.

"They are. I never get enough." Laureen put just the slightest quiver into the final word.

Giles shot upright immediately, watching her closely. "What is it, my love?"

How long did she have to wait for maximum impact? She took a deep breath and let it out slowly, a soft note of sadness brushing the air. "Oh, nothing."

He moved as if the years were nothing, instantly at her feet as he looked into her eyes with concern. "Now, darling. No secrets between us."

"You keep plenty of secrets from me," she declared, fighting her amusement to keep the façade of sadness in place.

"Only when I think the secrets will make you happy down the road," he promised.

"Charmer."

"*Your* charmer," he insisted. Then in a typical Giles move, he swept her up and resettled in the chair, this time with her on his lap. "Now tell me what's got your sweet expression sliding into a frown of worry."

Laureen didn't push it—she was a good actress, but Giles was no fool. She fed him her prepared story.

"With Giles Jr. and Glenda away for over a year, it's going to be a little lonelier for me. Oh, I know I have you"—

she laid a hand on his chest in honest adoration—"but the grandchildren are so caught up in their own plans. Especially now that they've been given more responsibility with the company."

"They're good workers," Giles told her proudly. "Going to do amazing things for Borealis Gems. All of them are so strong and gifted in their jobs."

"They are. They take after their father, and their father's father." She tapped him briefly on the nose and watched his grin bloom at her playfulness. Then she sighed softly. "But all work and no play is a bad idea, Giles. It took a long time for me to teach you to relax. And Glenda is the one who makes sure our son takes time to smell the roses. Who is going to be there to help our grandsons realize there's more to life than a bottom line?"

Giles blinked. "Oh."

She snuggled against his broad chest, the way she had for years and years. While there she marveled a little that this sweet, determined polar bear shifter who had won her heart had no idea she could read him like a book.

"Well, work *is* important," Giles began.

"Work is *very* important," she agreed. "I couldn't want more for the company than to have our grandsons in charge. But if it means that they keep pushing off falling in love and starting their own families, well, then." She snapped upright, not just acting but sharing the truth she felt to her core. "I'd give the entire business to Midnight Inc. and be done with it if Borealis Gems proves to be a detriment to Cooper, Alex and James finding mates and forever loves."

Giles chuckled at her tone. "You're magnificent when you're fired up."

"It's just that I love you so much," she said honestly. "You're my heart, Giles Borealis, and don't you forget it."

"I love you, Laureen Borealis, and you leave the boys to me. I think I can deal with your worries easy enough," he promised.

~

AND HE HAD, OR SO IT APPEARED.

Giles didn't need to be reminded about the times she'd spent with Kaylee and James when they were younger, guiding the two youngsters into a rich, deep relationship that would be ready to bloom at the perfect moment.

There wasn't a reason to mention that Laureen had first met the Lazuli family years earlier, back at college. That she'd encouraged the parents to move to Yellowknife in the first place.

And when Lara had gone away to college, Laureen had kept in touch with the Orion pack through monthly "book club" visits with Amethyst Lazuli. Oh, yes, there'd been behind the scenes work done all around to be sure when Lara returned, she'd find a place to call home with Alex.

And the bits of help she might have provided Amber to make sure that she was ready to meet her challenge—well, that had simply been a woman helping another woman find her feet in the wilderness of the north.

Laureen glanced again at the pages of Giles's journal.

It was tempting to post a sticky note. To add a couple of lines referring to the items *she'd* set in motion, but then again, this wasn't about who had done what.

Her grandsons were mated. That's what counted. It had taken some doing, but every bit had been worth it. Giles was happy, she now had granddaughters, and soon there would be great-grandbabies to cuddle.

He didn't need to know the rest of the story.

Contented, she pressed a kiss to his lips.

Giles smiled without opening his eyes. "What a wonderful dream I'm having."

"Not a dream. Just an everyday, ordinary event," she whispered.

That made him pop awake. He pulled her into his lap, this shifter with whom she'd spent most of her life. He stared at her face, fingers brushing her cheek gently. "A kiss from you is far from ordinary, my love. You've magic in you, and it teases my senses and fills my soul with joy."

"Sweet talker." But she leaned closer and kissed him again because good behavior should be rewarded.

He hummed happily.

"He adores you so much."

The voice in her head that was Giles, but not, was as familiar to her as breathing. *"I adore him too. And you as well, sweet bear of mine."*

"Of course you adore me. I'm the best of bears, after all. I'm the one who knew you were ours before he did."

"Smart, beautiful bear," Laureen agreed.

"And cute. Don't forget cute," Giles's bear prompted before offering the equivalent of a kiss to her nose.

"You two stop flirting," Giles said, but it wasn't a complaint. It was joy and forever and family.

Laureen felt contentment to the tips of her toes. Grandchildren who were happy, children living rich lives, and the heart of her heart *and* his bear staring at her with love.

She couldn't have arranged it better if she'd tried.

~

New York Times Bestselling Author Vivian Arend
brings you a light-hearted paranormal trilogy
Borealis Bears

Get mated—or else!

When the meddling, match-making family patriarch lays
down the law, Giles Borealis' three polar bear shifter
grandsons agree to follow his edict. Only James, Alex and
Cooper each have a vastly different plan in mind to deal
with their impending mating fevers. Will any of them be
able to fight fate?

Spoiler: *not likely!*

~

Borealis Bears
The Bear's Chosen Mate
The Bear's Fated Mate
The Bear's Forever Mate

~

ABOUT THE AUTHOR

With over 2.5 million books sold, Vivian Arend is a *New York Times* and *USA Today* bestselling author of over 60 contemporary and paranormal romance books, including the Six Pack Ranch and Granite Lake Wolves.

Her books are all standalone reads with no cliffhangers. They're humorous yet emotional, with sexy-times and happily-ever-afters. Vivian pretty much thinks she's got the best job in the world, and she's looking forward to giving readers more HEAs. She lives in B.C. Canada with her husband of many years and a fluffy attack Shih-tzu named Luna who ignores everyone except when treats are deployed.

www.vivianarend.com

Made in the USA
Las Vegas, NV
02 December 2021

35831065R00111